Split
SKIRT

Split SKIRT

Agnes Rossi

Random House
New York

Library of Congress Cataloging-in-Publication Data
Rossi, Agnes.
Split skirt / Agnes Rossi.—1st ed.
p.   cm.
ISBN 0-679-42543-8
1. Female offenders—United States—Fiction. 2. Women—United States—Fiction.
I. Title.
PS3568.084694S68   1994
813'.54—dc20   93-26887

Book Design by Tanya M. Pérez

Manufactured in the United States of America
24689753
First Edition

FOR MY SISTERS

Split
SKIRT

ONE

I'll never forget the day Bess Myerson was arrested. Poor Bess, a former Miss America, the cultural-affairs director for the city of New York, caught stealing $44.07 worth of merchandise from a discount store. When the detective emptied her purse—they always do that, dump your bag on their crummy metal desks—he found $160 in cash. The women in my circle were shocked and saddened. I pretended to feel the same way. What I actually felt was relief. Misery loves company. I've been a shoplifter for thirty years, and today, in exactly one hour, I'm going to jail for it.

My husband wanted to see if he could use his influence with the judge who sentenced me. John is very well connected. God knows, he's pulled strings before.

Not this time, John, I insisted.

Agnes Rossi

This time I face the music.

On my night table is a bank envelope containing five $100 bills. I open the envelope, pull out the bills, fold each one in half the long way. With my sharp embroidery scissors I snip the stitches that run along the waistband of the cheap brown pants I bought yesterday. I pull back the fabric and discover a nice thick strip of elastic. Good! I slide the folded bills along the elastic, then tuck it back in place. My fingers tremble as I stitch the seam closed, hold the pants up to the light, inspect my handiwork. Satisfied that my stash of money is nearly undetectable, I fold the pants and add them to the clothes I've already packed in my red canvas bag.

I could leave now, drive very slowly, take back roads. No. I certainly don't want to be early. I sit down on my bed, hold my bag on my lap.

The next time I see my bedroom I'll be back home again, safe and sound, the three days over. How I love this room. Pale blue and rich cream. It took me two years to find this oak furniture. My mother would faint if she knew what I paid for it. Here in this room, more than anywhere else in my house, I feel how far I've come from the apartment in Atlantic City where I grew up.

My daughter's room, opposite ours, is clean and vacant. Susan is away at school. She left in September, and I miss her more than I can say. I open her closet door, run my hand along the clothes she left behind. I pull a book from her shelf, thumb its pages. Susan doesn't know I'm going to jail, and she never will, if I can help it. My husband and I have agreed that if she calls while I'm gone, he'll tell her I'm off on one of my spa vacations. It'll work. John will be his usual distracted self, and Susan won't press.

Between the living and dining rooms I stop, bounce my bag against my knee. We used to entertain a lot, John's business associates mostly. I remember satin evening skirts, big bowls of

4

SPLIT SKIRT

salad greens chilling on the back porch, separating husbands and wives when I did the seating charts. After everybody had gone, I'd undress in my bedroom, put on my nightgown to the sound of caterers cleaning up in the kitchen. I don't miss dinner parties or cocktail parties or Christmas open houses, but these rooms seem to.

The doors to my husband's study are closed. I push one open, half expect to find John at his desk, bifocals down low on his nose. "Y-e-e-e-s?" he'd say playfully. John is away on business; he made a point to be out of town today, I encouraged him to go. Above the couch hangs a black-and-white photograph of my mother-in-law on her wedding day. The French lace, the flowers, the headpiece and veil all seem to make Lorraine uneasy. She looks ready to put on street clothes and get down to the business of being married to money.

Thank God you didn't live to see this, Lorraine. You would be livid. A Tyler going to jail? Not if you had anything to say about it.

A chill goes through me, I turn away. Rest in peace, Lorraine. Try to, anyway.

It's time to head out to the car now. House keys, car keys, check the burners on the stove. I hit the button to activate the alarm, have thirty seconds to get out.

The garage smells of gasoline and grass clippings. My car, a full-size Cadillac, welcomes me. The youngest of my three sons, Andrew, hates this car. He lectures me about conspicuous consumption, my profligate use of fossil fuel. Andrew is twenty-five. He lives in Maine, can't keep a job, has all the answers. My shoplifting, he says, is a perfectly understandable response to consumerism. "It's not your fault, Mom. You've been taught to seek emotional gratification from material goods. Deep down, you resent that, so you strike back at the system, in this case the

5

department store. Simple as that." Beneath Andrew's arrogance, and his kind heart, is his need to understand why his mother steals things she could easily afford to buy.

That makes two of us, sweetie.

Better minds than Andrew's have explained my condition to me. Kleptomania, according to strict Freudians, is an extreme manifestation of penis envy. The majority of kleptomaniacs are women. We steal because we were born without penises. We are, in fact, out there stealing penis substitutes. More sensible mental health professionals believe kleptomania is a misguided defense mechanism, an attempt to ensure psychological survival. Kleptomaniacs steal when we are about to be anxious or depressed. I take a bracelet or scarf, I'm told, the way an alcoholic takes a drink.

In doctors' offices and libraries all over Bergen County, I listen, I read, I nod my head. Psychological theories, especially those that seem reasonable enough, flatten me. They make me feel stale, cantankerous. If a supreme being were the source of these theories, I'd be more receptive, but how is it that one mind, limited, mysterious even to itself, can interpret another?

I turn the key, step on the gas, think of Bess Myerson. She was up in Pennsylvania visiting her boyfriend in Allenwood Federal Prison; he was serving time for tax evasion. This man was twenty-three years Bess's junior; she'd taken him away from his wife and children. When visiting hours were over, Bess checked into a modest motel and spent the night. She got up the following morning, drove to the K mart or whatever it was, stole cheap sandals, earrings, nail polish, batteries. It must have been a very long night, Bess. You must have been desperate.

The engine is warm now.

It's time to go.

I put my car in reverse, ease out onto the street.

TWO

When I was sentenced to three days in the Bergen County jail for driving while intoxicated and possession of less than a quarter of a gram of cocaine, I didn't believe I'd really have to go. We'll appeal, I thought. I'll pay a monster fine, do community service, agree to attend A.A. for a year, anything. The fact that I was really going to jail didn't sink in until I was back in my lawyer's office after my hearing and he told me I'd be allowed to bring my own clothes. "And tone it down, Rita," Barry said. "No tight jeans, nothing like that. County jail is no place to show off, you hear me?"

Oh my God, I thought.

Oh. My. God.

. . .

Into my knapsack go gray sweatpants, two oversize T-shirts, plain white underwear—briefs, not bikinis. Yesterday I looked at the underwear in my drawer—black lycra, hand-painted paisley on raw silk, little red stars on a background of cobalt blue—and remembered Barry's advice. I walked over to the dusty old clothing store on Maywood Avenue and bought a three-pack of Hanes cotton briefs.

Soap, deodorant, toothpaste, toothbrush. With my knapsack open and giving off its usual smell—a bottle of Obsession cracked on the way home from my honeymoon in Aruba three years ago—I calculate what I'll need for the days and nights I'll be gone. The Spartan quality of what I wind up with pleases me. No jewelry, no makeup, no lingerie. This is how a person might pack if she were going on retreat, which, it occurs to me, is exactly where I ought to be going.

"Come on, Rita," my husband shouts from the foot of the stairs. The screen door bangs as Alex, Kevin, and Marisol head out to the car. It's time, then. I pick up my knapsack and stop for a moment in front of the mirror, wanting a word with myself before I leave. "Just hold on," I say as loudly as I dare. "Take it one minute at a time. Three days from now all of this will be over."

I wish I believed that.

There's a shine in my eyes, a preternatural glow like when I've been up all night getting high.

In the car I'm so scared I can't get a deep breath. I taste iron, as if I've held rusty scissors, then put my fingers in my mouth.

Kevin and Marisol sit in the backseat, spooked by their father's silence. In the side-view mirror I can see Kevin resting his head against the window. He's a handsome kid, with Alex's straight nose and strong chin, his mother's dark hair and olive skin. I imagine our eyes meeting, imagine Kevin giving me a sweet, conspiratorial smile. Not a chance. In Kevin's mind, I've gone from inconsequential to vulgar.

Marisol unbuckles her seat belt. She's small enough at seven to slip between the two front seats and rest her head on her father's shoulder. Her fingers fumble with Alex's ear, his chin, then come to rest, splayed, on his cheek. My fingers itch to push her head away, replace it with my own. Marisol is a little girl, I remind myself, and these last few weeks haven't been easy on any of us. Her eyes are glassy, the hair at the nape of her neck is tangled.

Am I imagining it, or is Alex driving more carefully than usual? He is. He's obeying the speed limit, using his turn signals self-consciously, like a teenager taking his road test. Ordinarily Alex doesn't bother with blinkers unless he's making a particularly disruptive left turn or cutting somebody off. But today, apparently, one criminal in our family's enough.

We head down a steep hill. The momentum makes me feel how unnatural surrender is. I've been ordered to appear at this place on this date, and I'm complying, even though my instincts, my insides, chant no.

We're here. We are here. The Bergen County jail sits on a busy street. I expected to drive down an access road, long and pitted, the kind that jostles hard, gets your shoulder blades going. The building is unrelentingly institutional, square and squat. There are flowers planted on either side of the walkway leading to the door.

Do I kiss Alex before I get out? He didn't shave this morning, so there's just enough stubble to make a good kiss bracing. I want him to reach for me with both arms, squeeze hard, tell me in my ear that he loves me. He looks over at me like I'm a hitchhiker he's letting out at a light, takes my chin between thumb and index finger, kisses me on the forehead. The forehead. I should have bolted the second the car stopped.

My watch, wallet, wedding ring, and house keys are taken from me and dropped into a manila envelope. The envelope is sealed, tagged, and added to a row of identical envelopes.

In a small room that's tiled like a shower stall, a guard watches me undress. "Bend over," she says, then shoves a latex-covered finger inside me once, then again. I tell myself this is no worse than my annual gynecological exam.

Another guard pulls each piece of clothing out of my knapsack, shakes it, drops it back in. I smell perfume. The guard sniffs, sniffs again, rolls her eyes. "You shouldn't have," she says.

As I'm led through open areas and down long hallways, I feel a weird itchiness inside that tells me how soft I am compared to how hard it is here. The edges of cement steps are rounded, the iron bars rusted, the paint faded and peeling. The stench is a blend of sour cigarette smoke, cafeteria food, and the worst body odor I've ever smelled—not just from armpits, but crotches too. Every person I see looks disturbed—bad wigs, short pants, eyelids that flutter.

My cell is a grim little room, three cinder-block walls, iron bars, cement floor, two cots, a tiny sink, and a toilet. Here, at least, I'm out of reach. Anybody who wants to get at me has to unlock the door first. Barry told me I'd probably have to share a cell, but there's no sign of anybody yet. Please let me have this cell to myself. Three days alone here might not be so bad . . . except how in the world will I use that toilet in plain view of the guards and prisoners walking past? Maybe things settle down here at night. I could wait until then, I could . . . my eyes burn and then fill.

Is this it for me now? Have I hit bottom? People say so-and-so landed in jail; have I? Landed, that is. I open my knapsack, root around for my brush, find it but don't use it. A particularly surly-looking prisoner is going by, and I don't want to call attention to myself.

The same guard who brought me here puts her key in the lock, pushes the door open, and says, "After you."

In walks a woman who looks about fifty.

My cellmate, damn it.

She's neatly dressed, in navy-blue slacks and a white cotton pullover. Her light brown hair is set and sprayed.

"Hello," she says. "I'm Mrs. Tyler."

Mrs. Tyler. In jail? Maybe she's not my cellmate—maybe she's a social worker or a volunteer of some kind? She offers me her hand like she's the president of a classy women's club and I'm a prospective member.

The guard looks at us wryly, says, "Lunch at eleven-thirty, ladies," and locks us in.

Mrs. Tyler puts her red canvas bag on the other cot, then sits down beside it. She looks at my knapsack and says, "Is today your first day too?"

"Yes. I just got here."

"How long are you . . . how long is your sentence?"

"Three days. I get out Monday morning."

"Same here," Mrs. Tyler says, smiling weakly.

I nod, turn away, open my knapsack, and take out my book. I brought only one, *Wuthering Heights,* in the hope I'd be able to lose myself in it as I did when I was twenty and read it in one day, alone in my parents' house. Before packing my copy to come here, I tore the front cover off so as not to tempt the ire of the other prisoners who I imagined would be irritated by a white girl reading a serious book.

Mrs. Tyler stands up, looks like she'd pace if pacing were possible in so small a space. She's rounded in a way that's easy to look at, cheeks and forearms and butt. Her clothes look expensive but dreary, the sad eunuch look of Brooks Brothers for women. Her face is pretty—clear blue eyes, a perfect little nose. Her skin is pink and the texture is fine; she's been careful in the sun. She wraps her fingers around one of the bars, then opens her hand, checks it for dirt. She catches me watching her and stiffens.

"Where are you from, Rita?" she says.

"Here. Maywood. I've lived in New Jersey all my life."

"I have as well. I grew up in Atlantic City. I live in Saddle River now."

Saddle River? Richard Nixon lives there, Alan Alda. Women from Saddle River don't go to jail. But, then, neither do women from Maywood, generally, and here I am.

I'm dying to know what she's in for but don't know how to ask without sounding like a character in a 1940s prison movie. Is she a drunk driver like me? Do they pair prisoners up by their crimes? She doesn't really look like a drinker. No burst capillaries. Her voice is smooth and steady, not loopy or scratchy.

This mattress feels like it's filled with wet sand; it reminds me of the futon I slept on for a couple of years. The first time Alex stayed over at my apartment, he tossed and turned all night, could barely straighten up in the morning. That very afternoon he bought a Beautyrest over the phone. Here is a man who means business, I thought. Here is a man.

Last night Alex didn't get home until almost two o'clock. When I heard his key in the front door, I got out of bed, crept to the top of the stairs. He went straight into the kitchen, picked up the phone, dialed, spoke very softly. I couldn't make out his words, but I recognized the fervor in his voice.

Five years ago, when Alex and I fell in love, he used to call me twenty minutes after he left my apartment, exactly as long as it took him to drive home. He'd tell me that he missed me already, wanted to hear my voice. He could taste me in his mustache, he'd say, he could smell me on his fingers. He'd tell me what he was going to do to me the next time we were alone. Go to sleep, angel, he'd say. Sweet dreams.

A woman starts screaming, something about five thousand dollars, motherfucker, cocksucker. She's going to kill the bastard when she gets out. "Tear . . . him . . . up." Her shrieks are guttural, phlegmy, raw.

I sit up, pinch my lip, try to think of something other than the screaming. Mrs. Tyler stares at me, her gaze like a hand I don't want on my shoulder. The screamer is told to shut up by other prisoners and then by a guard. "Shut your fucking mouth." Something, a billy club maybe, is run along the bars. The shrieks soften, then fade. The screamer weeps.

"Well, at least she's quieter," Mrs. Tyler says.

Her voice is reassuring. It reminds me that seventy-two hours from now we'll be back out in the world.

"Are you married, Rita?" Mrs. Tyler asks.

"Yes."

"Any children?"

"My husband has two from his first marriage, a boy and a girl. They live with us. What about you?"

"I've been married for thirty-four years. I have four children, three sons and a daughter. Nobody knows I'm here, except my husband, of course. His name is John. My husband's name is John."

I nod, can't think of anything else to say. I'm about to go back to my book when Mrs. Tyler says, "Do you have brothers or sisters?"

"Seven sisters," I say.

Her eyes widen and warm. She smiles. "You're Catholic, then," she says.

I nod, foregoing my usual "I was raised Catholic," which seems, suddenly, adolescent.

"And where are you in the seven?"

"Eight. There are eight girls all together. I have seven sisters. I'm in the middle, three older, four younger."

She nods. "I come from a big family too. I have one sister and four brothers. I was the oldest."

There are no windows here. The lighting is dim and yellowish like in a bus station or hospital corridor. The screamer, the weeper now, is crying like a child who only wants to make noise. Mrs. Tyler looks toward the sound, closes her eyes for a moment.

"Oldest daughters in Irish families were born servants," she says. "Scrubbing floors, peeling potatoes, and there was always a baby. My mother worked nights in a commercial laundry." She secures the sheet at the foot of her cot, making two perfect hospital corners.

Her mother worked in a laundry, and now she lives in Saddle River? That's quite a leap. I hear elements of both worlds in her voice. Liveliness tempered or roughness refined. I wait to see if she's going to talk any more. Ten or fifteen seconds pass before I say, "So, Mrs. Tyler, what are you in for?"

THREE

Shoplifting, Rita.
        Retail theft.

I was arrested three times in three months. The judge at my trial looked down at me and said, "What am I going to do with you, Mrs. Tyler?" At that critical moment I smiled. I didn't mean to, I swear, I was as shocked and disapproving as anybody. Judge Keller was not amused. "Three days in county jail," he said and slammed his gavel down.

I've had this problem for years and years, since before you were born, probably, but this binge was by far my worst. I felt as if I were hurtling toward something or somewhere, and I couldn't stop until I got there. This place, it turns out, is where I was headed.

I have a good life, an easy life. I should be grateful. Most of my time is spent on diversions. I shop, I travel, I attend lectures, I volunteer. I paint flowers on small wooden plaques. I have a housekeeper and a gardener and a husband who is away a great deal. My children are grown.

When I go to sleep at night, there are seven empty bedrooms in my house. Seven. All made up. Children leave. You raise them to be independent, and believe me, you're glad when they go. Your house is your own, finally. You don't have these know-it-alls telling you what is what all the time. John junior, my oldest son, lives on the Upper East Side of Manhattan, not far away. David's in California. Andrew in Maine.

Susan, my youngest, started college in September, Brown University. I drove her up there myself. We loaded the car with boxes and the old-fashioned trunk I insisted she let me buy for her. I had it inscribed with her initials, which made her groan. "This isn't 1958, Ma, or 1908. I'm not going off on a tour of Europe." S.B.T. Susan Brennan Tyler. Girls who go off to college get trunks, period.

I so much hoped we'd have a good trip, one we'd remember, a rite of passage, but the truth is, we were both on edge. I wanted it to be how I wanted it to be; Susan had her own ideas. She was nervous—it was a new place, so many strangers. Susan is brash only with me; with other people she is deferential, sweet. Her anxiety made her snippy. I suggested we stop for lunch, but Susan wasn't hungry. I made polite conversation with her roommate, a girl from northern California who'd come east unescorted; Susan telegraphed apologies to her and hustled me out of there. In the bank, half as a joke, I asked if she'd like to order the checks with the rainbows or teddy bears printed on them. My God, she looked at me as if I'd suggested she wear a sailor suit to freshman orientation the following day. Walking me to my car, she softened. "Be careful driving," she said. "I'll call you soon."

I was numb as I found my way back to the interstate. Yes, well, I started to feel really awful. Mind or body, it's hard to say. My palms were damp on the wheel, my heart was racing. I was going sixty miles an hour but felt as if I was barely moving. I kept looking at my reflection in the rearview mirror; that steadied me. I was at once proud and envious of my only daughter. Nineteen and spending her first night in the dorm of an Ivy League college. I drove with the fingers of my left hand out the window to feel the rush of cold air.

A few miles into Connecticut I spotted a shopping mall from the highway. I saw the big round *M* of Macy's, so welcoming. I got off at the next exit, circled back, and found the mall without having to stop and ask for directions. I stole a gorgeous charcoal-gray blazer, severe and sophisticated. In it I look like a lady poet.

FOUR

A buzzer sounds, loud and low-pitched. Its vibrations run down my spine, and Mrs. Tyler says, "Do you suppose that means it's lunchtime?" I close my book and look through the bars to see if anybody's coming to let us out. Women stream past. One of them—she limps, wears a tight blue workshirt— pulls our door open as she goes by. Mrs. Tyler and I say thank you in unison.

Out in the hall, in the crowd of women, I feel protective of Mrs. Tyler. I may be out of place here, but Mrs. Tyler, with her white Tretorn sneakers and mild blue eyes, she's from another planet entirely.

The cafeteria is huge and dingy. Barry said male prisoners outnumber female twenty to one here. The shared facilities—the cafeteria, the yard, the dayroom—sometimes hold as many as a thousand men. Fifty women can't fill even one corner. The cavernous feel gives me vertigo. There are guards at every door.

I stand back to let Mrs. Tyler go first in line. She hands me a tray and takes one for herself. We're given meat loaf, mashed potatoes, white bread smeared with margarine, orange drink. I choose one of the dozens of empty tables. Mrs. Tyler offers me her ketchup packet, which I accept gratefully. The food is lukewarm and tastes waterlogged.

Barry said inmates in county jail are a mixed bag. People arrested for vagrancy or drunk-and-disorderly alongside felons and repeat offenders. You'd almost be better off doing real time, he said; that way you have a shot at a minimum-security facility. In county jail you've got defendants waiting for bail to be set, or worse, the ones who can't make bail in there for months on end, years sometimes. It's drugs that land people here more than anything else—serious drugs, possession with the intent to distribute. Some prostitutes, maybe, from the truckstops and cheap motels, but they're in and out, usually.

Keep to yourself, Rita, he said. You think you're tough, but believe me, compared with the girls in County, you're an absolute angel. Whatever you do, don't mouth off. Jail is no joke. People get hurt.

I keep my eyes lowered at first, but gradually I realize that nobody's paying any attention to Mrs. Tyler or me. Several women are staring morosely at their food, but most are involved in conversations. Some talk without stopping, talk and talk and talk. Many seem to be telling stories about arguments they've had, confrontations. I told him, I told her. The affront in their voices carries. They gesture emphatically, shake their heads. I wouldn't have thought fifty-odd women could make so much noise.

SPLIT SKIRT

Many are dolled up, eye shadow, mascara, blush, nail polish, braided hair, lined lips. I'm surprised, but I shouldn't be. These are women with time on their hands and access to beauty aids.

Another buzzer sounds. We line up and are herded into a recreation room. There's a big TV in one corner, metal chairs strewn around, some of them upended, and three pay phones, with a line of women waiting to use each one.

Rules are scrawled on the wall by the phones in uneven black letters. I can see brushstrokes in the paint. WAIT YOUR TURN. COLLECT CALLS ONLY. THREE MINUTE MAX. Most callers stay on past the limit, hang up only when the guard snaps her fingers and says, "Let's go."

My turn finally comes. The phone at home rings four, five, six times. Just as the operator suggests I try again later, Alex picks up and accepts the charges. At the sound of his voice my knees weaken.

"Rita?" he says.

He's worried about me, he's glad I called.

I mean to begin slowly, to tell him I'm okay, that jail isn't so bad, but the tender way he said my name makes my heart ache. I get right to the point.

"Where were you last night, Alex?"

"What?"

"I want to know where you were last night."

"Out."

"Out where?"

"Just out. Rita, are you all right? How is it there so far?"

"You were with Lee, weren't you, Alex?"

"What are you talking about? No. I went out with Jerry, we had a couple of beers."

"You're lying. I know you're lying."

No response. I can hear the dishwasher running in the background at home, I can hear a baseball game on the radio that sits on our kitchen counter.

"I was awake when you came in, Alex. I heard you make a phone call. Who were you calling?"

"We are not having this conversation now, Rita, do you understand?"

"No, I don't understand. Why won't you just answer me?"

Silence, again.

The guard snaps her fingers, takes a step toward me. My three minutes can't possibly be up, but I'm certainly not going to argue with her.

"Listen to me, Rita," Alex says. "Be careful in there. Concentrate on taking care of yourself, will you please?"

I walk the perimeter of the room, arms folded under my chest. Am I going to lose Alex now? Have I already lost him? My stomach, my heart, my blood—everything plummets. Alex is an extremist—he's yours or he's not—and he's capable of cruel resolve. I press hard against my ribs and envision an orderly single life, the kind I never lived, with a small apartment, sparsely furnished, no clutter, a place where I'll spend long afternoons reading and drinking good coffee. How can I be both terrified and tempted?

Mrs. Tyler is sitting against the back wall, just where I left her. She's working hard to project amiable indifference, exactly as I would if she left me alone in the midst of the others. I'm minding my own business here, her expression says, not looking for trouble. As I get close, she taps the metal chair next to hers.

I sit down beside her and take a deep breath. What is Alex doing right this second? After hanging up the phone, he probably walked out into the backyard and is standing there now with his hands in his pockets. He's looking in this direction, toward the jail, and hoping I'll have enough sense to behave myself here. When his concern for my welfare threatens to weaken his resolve, he'll remind himself that all of this is my own damn fault.

"Is everything okay at home, Rita?" Mrs. Tyler asks.

I mean to blow her off, tell her yes, yes, everything's fine. But then I turn to her and see that she isn't just being polite. There is the most inviting light in her eyes, a mix of curiosity and patience. What the hell, I tell myself, she's a lot older than I am, she's been married a long time, maybe she knows something.

"I'm pretty sure my husband is having an affair with his ex-wife," I say.

Mrs. Tyler doesn't flinch. She stands up, repositions her chair so that we're sitting face-to-face, and waits.

I find myself formulating a version of the story to tell her, editing out parts I know she'll disapprove of, slanting other parts my way. Fatigue derails this effort. I'm always giving people versions of things, and I'm tired of it. I'm going to try telling the truth for a change.

FIVE

*I*t's a long story, Mrs. Tyler. I'm not even sure where to begin. I've been feeling bad for a long time. Months and months. Out of sorts, out of sync. Something's wrong with me, and I don't know what it is. I'm angry, God, I'm fucking furious, but at who or what I can't say exactly. I'm afraid maybe I have a mood disorder, something clinical, like manic depression. I could have a chemical imbalance, and all I need is a steady dose of lithium—or is it librium? Maybe what I've got is terminal PMS, who the hell knows?

The weeks before I got arrested were particularly rough. I was impossible to live with, Alex could tell you that. He got the brunt of it. He'd leave his underwear on the bathroom floor or let his eyes wander while I was talking and I'd explode—yell, cry, storm out of the house. A couple of hours later I'd feel guilty and insecure, so I'd sit too close to him on the couch, hold his hand in the grocery store. I just made everything worse.

How do you know when you're having a nervous breakdown? I felt as if I were two people, a clingy little wife and a shrew. Neither one was me.

"What's the matter with you, Ri?" Alex would ask. "What is going on?"

I didn't have any answers for him.

The nights were the worst. I'd fall asleep much too early, exhausted from the day, then lie there wide awake at two or three. I'd get up, go downstairs and try to read. I started going outside for air, walking around the neighborhood wearing some combination of pajamas and whatever clothes Alex had left lying around the den.

One night I was walking up and down our street wearing pajama bottoms and a button-down shirt of Alex's. It smelled of perspiration and faded cologne. In that shirt I felt closer to Alex than I had in months. It was as much of him as I wanted next to me.

A cop stopped and asked if I was all right. Dressed as I was, I knew I looked deranged, so I said I was searching for my cat. She'd disappeared two days before, I told him, and my children missed her. He asked what she looked like. I said she was a tabby, even though I'm not sure what that means exactly, I just know it's a kind of cat. "Get in," he said. "We'll use my search-light."

Together we rode up and down a dozen streets. His spotlight was narrow but bright. He aimed it at people's garbage cans and into their backyards. I felt guilty for lying but loved sitting in the front seat of a police car. Have you ever been in one? They're wonderful, really; they seem weightier than regular cars. There's a rifle and a radar gun and the dispatcher's voice amidst plenty of static. The cat we were looking for didn't exist—so what? We were doing a general inspection, keeping an eye on things.

After twenty minutes or so, the cop said I shouldn't worry. Cats always come back eventually. "She's probably just off having a good time for herself."

He drove me back to my house. I wanted to ask him in for scrambled eggs and coffee but couldn't because Alex would have gotten up and I'd have had to say Officer so-and-so and I had been out looking for our cat, Martha. I had to give her a name, something to call out softly in the direction of the searchlight's beam.

A few days before I got arrested, I woke up at three o'clock in the morning. Moonlight poured in my bedroom windows. Alex usually pulls the shades when he comes to bed, but he'd forgotten or hadn't bothered. The whole room was filled with silvery light. Instead of getting up and going downstairs, I turned and looked at Alex. Watching him sleep, I asked myself how long I expected him to put up with me. Just how far did I think I could push him? I traced his eyebrows with my index finger, kissed his nose. If this marriage is important to you, I said to myself, you'd better start acting like it. I rubbed my forehead across Alex's chest, my feet against his feet. He put his arm around my waist and held me until I fell back to sleep.

For the next couple of days I was on my best behavior. I made a point of smiling at Alex when he came home in the evening, asked him how his day went, watched TV with him after dinner. We went to bed at the same time. I initiated sex because Alex says I don't do that enough and also because I wanted to feel as close to him as possible. Unfortunately, Alex chose to play hard to get. That is to say, he didn't return my affections wholeheartedly. He was a little stingy, paying me back for the weeks previous or, maybe, genuinely leery of my newfound good cheer.

The morning of the arrest, I put on a skirt I'd bought a few days before, one Alex hadn't seen. It was coffee-colored and short, much shorter than I usually wear, and it had a slit up the back. I put on a silk blouse, department-store pantyhose straight out of the package, and my best three-inch heels. I have nice legs—Alex is a big fan of my legs. It seems shallow and stupid to me now, thinking I could vamp it up at the breakfast table, get back in Alex's good graces by reminding him what a hot number I am. My sunny disposition hadn't gotten his attention; maybe six inches of thigh would.

Walking across the kitchen, I felt shy, thought Alex would know I was flirting with him. He looked up from his cereal and said, "That skirt's too short."

"It is not. Skirts are shorter now."

"It looks cheap."

"Give me a break," I said and sat down across from him.

He dropped his spoon into his bowl and said, "I don't have time for your bullshit this morning, Rita. Wear whatever you want." He got up and walked out, left half his breakfast behind.

I wish I'd said, Alex, I'm trying to get your attention. I'm coming on to you, for Christ's sake.

The rest of the day was strange and feverish. It seemed to have a trip wire running down the middle of it. I walked into work feeling the effects of the morning's humiliation. It wasn't even nine o'clock. Already I'd attempted to seduce my husband and failed.

All morning my head was swimmy. I couldn't look right at people for fear they'd see craziness in my eyes. I went out for a walk at lunch. Walking helps. If I keep moving, I don't feel the jitters quite so much. Two things happened while I was out. First

SPLIT SKIRT

I cashed my paycheck, something I never do. Ordinarily I give my check to Alex. He pays the bills, and I get whatever money I need at a cash machine. That day I had some half-baked notion I'd go out and blow a chunk of money, buy a couple of pairs of very expensive shoes and give Alex whatever was left. When the teller handed me the envelope, I didn't put it in my wallet, didn't even put it in my purse. I stuck nearly eight hundred dollars in the pocket of my skirt. I liked the way the lump of money felt against my hipbone.

I left the bank and walked down the street past a deli. Out front a little Chinese girl was refusing to go inside. Her father was trying to make her. She wore a pink dress with a bib collar, white ankle socks, and black patent-leather Mary Janes. I stopped on the sidewalk to watch. Her father towered over her, barking one Chinese word over and over, pointing at the door. She shook her head no, was as fixed as a fire hydrant. He opened the door; I smelled salami and vinegar and burned coffee; she turned her head slowly, surveyed the street calmly, regally, as if there might be someplace out there she'd consider going. Her self-possession took my breath away. Her father lunged at her, grabbed her by the arm, yanked her inside. She went, of course—her feet weren't touching the ground—but her expression didn't change. Her face was resolute even as she got carried off.

I stood there a minute celebrating the little girl's strength of will, her calm in the face of her father's fury. She had refused to back down, for love.

When I got back to the office, six or seven women were gathered around the receptionist's desk. One of them waved me over before I was even off the elevator. "Read this," she said.

It was a memo outlawing split skirts, those things we used to call culottes that reappeared a few years ago. The president was dismayed—that's what it said, "dismayed"—to see certain staff

29

members wearing what looked like shorts to him. He understood these garments were called split skirts. Some of them, he admitted, were more acceptable than others, but since he didn't want to have to rule on every case, all split skirts were disallowed. He trusted we understood that our business depends on our projecting a professional image. Split skirts are not in keeping with that goal.

The receptionist, a tall blonde named Dolores, leaned back in her chair and crossed her long legs. "Is Mr. Hall going to come around to check if there's a seam between our legs? If he finds one, do we get to go home?"

I'm an account manager for a company that does recruitment advertising—employment ads, help wanted. The son of the man who started the company runs it now. Mr. Hall is about sixty, benevolent, paternal, a father who takes pleasure in his sons' high-spiritedness but expects his daughters to be demure. The senior people, all men, are rakish types, arrogant individualists. Women get ahead by being drudges. The ones who keep a low profile, speak softly after a moment's thought, and dress conservatively get promoted. All of the big national clients, the ones who buy splashy display ads in the Sunday *Times,* are handled by men. Women take care of the small businesses, strictly in-column stuff. I've tried to fight it, too hard, probably. I speak up at meetings and question assignments, but I'm not doing too well. My work is often criticized or ignored. Some of the men exchange looks when I open my mouth. Lately I've been tempering my behavior because I'm making decent money and I need this job. I've been trying to talk less and listen more. I mimic the facial expressions of the other women at meetings. The look is one of hesitant gratitude. Our being at the table is enough. I used to think Mr. Hall hired only mealymouthed women. Now I suspect he creates them.

SPLIT SKIRT

Split skirts. No doubt his dismay was genuine.

No other account executives were out in the lobby. I knew I should act like a manager, not like a secretary—smile blandly and get the hell out of there, but Dolores looked so appealing slouching down in her chair. She usually arches her back, sticks her ass out in back and her chest out in front. Dolores must have been a big wearer of split skirts. She was furious and insisted we all go out for a drink at five o'clock.

I clearly wasn't one of them, I'd never even joined them for lunch, but now I wanted to go. Alex's rejecting me and my legs, the tyrannical Chinese father, a man dictating a memo outlawing split skirts—I'd had it. I'd thought I might take a long drive after work, get on Route 80 and head west, but I was leery of being alone with my thoughts. What I wanted to do was get drunk with a gang of women, drunk the way you imagine it will be before you do it, drunk and out from under.

The bar we went to smelled of gin and candle smoke and men's cologne. It had heart, this bar. "Mack the Knife" was playing on the jukebox, and my vodka and tonic tasted so good. The other women were talking shop, and since I wasn't part of their skirmishes, I was free to sip my drink, sing along with Bobby Darin, Mick Jagger, and Elvis, and admire my legs, which were crossed so that a good bit of thigh showed.

As I was ordering my third drink, a man joined our conversation. The bartender ushered him in. He was Latino, with round features, close-set eyes, lively as hell. The color in his cheeks didn't seem to come from drinking but from genuine enthusiasm. He charmed the whole group of us, made us laugh, did a routine about people in bars on Friday evenings. "You," he said to Dolores, "you're single, and maybe you have to go home and take a shower, change your clothes, meet somebody, but you don't really want to because, what the hell, you're already out and the water's fine.

"And you," he said to me, "you're married and maybe you and the old man had a fight this morning, so you said fuck you, Morton, I'm going out with the girls. You didn't even call him to let him know you'd be late, did you?"

I shook my head.

"Paul Melendez," he said, taking my hand. "And you are?"

I said Rita, and he said, "Who looked like she stepped out of a dolce vita." He took a long pull on his drink, leaned in, and said, "You have that screw-my-life-I'm-out-tonight look in your eyes, Rita." He moved his arms as if he were swimming underwater. Paul was clearly more interested in me than he was in Dolores, evidence enough that he was a man of some sophistication, I thought. Maybe he was just intimidated by her. A lot of men are. She's larger than life, a girl giant, big hair, long nails, bright colors. She looks like she climbed down off a billboard.

We all drank a lot. I kept pulling twenties out of my pocket and buying rounds. Little by little, the others went home. When Dolores left she grinned and gave me the thumbs-up sign behind Paul's back. I remember going to the bathroom and looking at my watch while I sat on the toilet, knowing Alex would be seriously worried by now. Good, I thought, serves him right. I figured I might as well make trouble if I was going to make trouble. I decided to ask Paul if he knew where we could get some cocaine.

Before I met Alex, I used to do a fair amount of cocaine. It was part of most big nights out but seemed to have run its course. I knew a few people who got into serious trouble with it, went to rehab or didn't. The rest of us more or less outgrew it, but if you've ever liked cocaine, you'll always be susceptible to its appeal. You're watching the news, and there's a story about a big bust. You see bags of the stuff, and even though you're home setting the table, maybe, or bundling newspapers to be recycled, you think, wow . . . look at all that. Whenever I get drunk I want some.

So I asked Paul, and he said, "Oh, yes," and off we went to get it. I climbed into his olive-green Plymouth Duster. He started it, turned to me and said, "I have five cars. Every one's a piece of shit."

We went to New York. I gave him a hundred dollars and stayed in the car, and he was gone for what seemed like an hour, long enough for me to sober up a bit and ask myself what the hell I was doing in a stranger's car in the middle of Harlem at ten o'clock at night. I remember putting on lipstick to give myself something to do.

Back in Jersey, in the bathroom of the Sheraton lounge in Englewood, I flushed the toilet and snorted two little spoons, flushed it again, snorted two more. Then I had a conversation with the attendant while I completely redid my makeup. She wasn't too receptive, but I didn't let that stop me. Even hostility can seem charming when you're freshly high.

I asked her if she was married, and she said she was. "It's hard, isn't it, keeping a marriage together?" "Very hard," she conceded. I told her it was just possible I'd made a big mistake getting married in the first place. There was a chance—"a very good chance"—I turned and looked dead at her as if she were a member of a jury and I was a lawyer presenting my closing argument—I wasn't cut out to be a wife.

"So get a divorce," she said, examining the hair on her arm.

I didn't believe a word of what I was saying, you understand. I was doing shtick.

Paul went to the men's room then, leaving me to sit up straight and gulp beer and feel better than I had in ages. When Paul came back he told me he'd been on his own since he was eight years old. His parents had shipped him out of Cuba when Castro came to power, put him on a plane for New York, where he was met by his oldest brother. It was the middle of winter, gray and sleeting. He looked around at Idlewild Airport and said, "What the fuck did I do, God?" His mother had told his brother how big Paul was so often that the brother threw his arms around the wrong kid. Over here, Paul had to say. Things didn't work out with the brother, and Paul wound up in an orphanage. The nuns let him run away because he was hard to handle, a bad influence on the other boys. "They encouraged me to escape," he said.

He looked so handsome telling his stories, like an actor alone on a stage, with just a wooden stool and a spotlight. He talked about women, how much he loved them, said he had a dream of finding his angel, the one who would make him perfectly happy. "Only a woman could do it," he said. He was a car salesman, talked about selling cars to rich people and ripping them off. "But," he said solemnly, raising one finger, "if you're P.B.P., protected by poverty, I give you a sweet deal, make it up on the next rich guy. I'm only one man."

I talked about Alex and the split-skirt memo and the little Chinese girl who wouldn't let herself be pushed around. We hated my boss together. Paul said he knew the type, rich white boys who glide through life. Dinosaurs, he said, fucking dodo birds.

I believed Paul and I were meant to sit in the corner of that hotel bar snorting cocaine and drinking ice-cold beer. Every so often I'd think of Alex, and a tremor would go through me. These failures in nerve were short-lived. The cocaine let me believe I didn't care what the consequences were, made me feel intact, integrated. If an eight-year-old could run away from an orphanage and be sitting next to me thirty years later, eyes bright, cheeks flushed, cigarette between thumb and index finger, maybe I could duck out of my life for a while and be okay.

SPLIT SKIRT

Paul and I were sitting side-by-side in a back booth. After a while we didn't bother going to the bathroom to do the coke anymore, we did it right there. Paul's thigh was touching mine, and there was a pleasant sort of electricity being generated at the contact point, but that seemed far from the most interesting thing happening at our table. I thought that was as far as it would go. Pretty stupid, I know. I'd left one bar with this man, bought drugs, gone to another bar where I'd talked at length about being unhappy in my marriage. We were leaning against one another, affirming over and over that we were kindred spirits. I had delusions of grandeur, thought Paul and I were into something more original than a pickup.

Then he took my hand and kissed each of my fingers, looked into my eyes, kissed me on the mouth.

What I felt most was a kind of exhaustion. The cocaine was just beginning to turn on me, and I was realizing I wasn't going to be able to get out of this easily.

Paul kissed my temple, my neck. He whispered, "Let's go upstairs, Rita."

While deciding what to do, I kissed Paul back, quite energetically, I have to admit, one hand on the back of his neck, the other on his thigh. I fell into my kissing mode. Finally, I got around to the business of saying no. I pulled back from the kiss and said, "I don't want to do this." Paul's demeanor changed in a split second. He looked slick and angry. "Give me a break," he said.

I said I was sorry and asked him to take me back to my car. He didn't argue. He took his hands off me and paid the bill. As we walked through the hotel lobby and out to the parking lot, I felt foolish in my short skirt and high heels: I knew exactly how I looked—drunk and dressed up.

Paul drove much too fast, slammed on the brakes at red lights, took corners on two wheels. I wished my head were clear, thought of a hundred things to say to test the water, but was too intimidated to open my mouth.

He pulled alongside my car, turned off the ignition, and looked over at me imploringly. He put his hands on my shoulders, dropped them down to my breasts, rubbed his palms over my nipples. I should have jumped out of the car right then, but I was still thinking I could negotiate this, make it so that Paul would understand. And his touch wasn't bullying, it was tentative, gentle. He opened my top button, slid his hand inside my bra, cupped my breast. I stiffened, said, "Paul, I told you I don't want to do this." My voice was breathy. I was still flirting. I didn't want him, but he should still want me. Another button, his other hand. My bra fastened in front. He opened it and I felt his breath on my nipples, then his lips and tongue.

I was about half coked-up resistance and half desire. I knew I had to get out of there or I'd have sex with this man in the parking lot of a bar after I'd told him no. He took one of my hands and rubbed it against his erection. I pulled free, put both hands on his shoulders, and pushed hard.

"No," I said.

He said it right back to me: "No."

All pretense of seduction disappeared. He put his left hand on my throat and pinned me against the seat. With his right hand he pulled up my skirt and grabbed at the waistband of my pantyhose.

"Lift up," he said, and when I didn't he started to choke me. I raised myself up off the seat, and while he was pulling my pantyhose and underwear down, I felt for the door handle with my right hand. I got it, waited until he was unbuckling his belt, and then I opened the door, leaned out, and screamed as loud as I could. Paul grabbed at my shirt, my hair, my neck. I just kept screaming, and finally I heard somebody shout, "Let her go."

SPLIT SKIRT

Two guys came running, two big boys, with broad shoulders and thick necks like college football players. The engine started, and I was shoved out of the car onto the macadam.

One of the boys chased Paul's car as far as the street. The other one kneeled down beside me and said, "Are you all right, ma'am?" My shirt and bra were open, my pantyhose and underwear down around my knees. He helped me up, then turned his back while I got myself together. He asked me if I wanted to call the police, said there was a telephone in the bar. The air was warm and I was sobbing, and this boy's voice was so serious. I remember thinking somebody had brought him up right. He put his hands in his pockets, looked off in the direction Paul had gone. He must have had a sister, this kid.

I told them I hadn't been raped, thanked them, said all I wanted to do was go home. They helped me into my car. The gentle one asked if I was all right to drive. "We can take you home," he said and then seemed to know I might be afraid to get in a car with two men, even his friend and him. "Or we can follow you. We don't have anything else to do, really."

I said thank you, no. They stood and watched while I started my car and pulled out. I saw them in my rearview mirror, standing shoulder-to-shoulder, and thought how lucky they were to be so big in the world, to have muscular arms to cross, to hear screams and be able to run toward them.

The side of my hip was badly scraped from when I got pushed out of the car, and my neck hurt, and I couldn't get the image of Paul unbuckling his belt with one hand out of my mind. His face had been blank, like somebody masturbating—single-minded, purposeful, devoid of emotion. His eyes had been swimmy, his mouth open. "Lift up," he'd said, and I had.

The cocaine high had worn off completely. All that was left was the hangover, the aftermath, an awful feeling, roaring anxiety mixed with self-loathing. What the hell was I doing? What was I going to say when I got home? It was after two. My pantyhose were torn in a dozen places. I'd take them off, I decided. Alex might not notice if I wasn't wearing any. I pulled them down, felt my scraped skin. How would I explain that? I was wriggling out of my stockings when I saw red lights in the rearview mirror.

I was stopped for going twenty in a forty-mile-an-hour zone. I didn't feel drunk anymore but knew I looked and probably smelled it. I thought about trying to hide what was left of the cocaine—the packet was in my purse—but the cop had his flashlight on me as he walked to my car. He took one look at me and told me to step out. He asked me to touch my fingers to my nose and say the alphabet backward. I can't do that even when I'm sober. He apologized as he put me in handcuffs. "Regulations," he said. "I understand," I said. It was my second ride in a police car, only this time I'm in the back, handcuffed.

At the station my pocketbook was searched. The cop seemed genuinely sorry when he pulled the little white packet out with two fingers. "What's this?" he said. He was mild-mannered, responsible, exactly the sort of person I always want to think well of me. On his desk he had a picture of his wife and son sitting in a small boat, waving. I imagined him alone at his desk, looking up at that picture and nodding, waving back, maybe, if he was in a certain mood.

"It's cocaine," I said, and he frowned, shook his head.

I called Barry, my lawyer. Barry called Alex.

I was videotaped taking the Breathalyzer. I watched the tape with Barry a few days later. It was a humbling experience. I'm trying my hardest to appear sober, but my eyes aren't quite focusing. My makeup is all smeared, and I keep looking at my watch as if this whole procedure is taking up too much of my valuable time. That tape was made just a half hour or so after I was assaulted. You'd never know it. I look drunk and disheveled, that's all.

Alex didn't say one word to me in the police station. He wouldn't even look at me. I was formally charged, then released on my own recognizance. Out in the car, Alex punched the steering wheel with both fists and said, "What the fuck, Rita?"

I told him I'd been upset about the way he'd treated me that morning. My voice was shaking, but I kept going. I said I'd gone out to a bar with some people from work, drank way too much, been talked into buying the cocaine.

Alex hates drugs. When we first got together, I told him I did a little cocaine once in a while; I thought he might want to try it. He said he didn't want anything to do with drugs, period, or with me if I was going to continue using them. Alex's vehemence seemed part of his general intensity then. I was already in love and hoping that would change my life. Giving up drugs seemed like a pretty good first step. Since then I'd fallen off the wagon a few times over the years, but not by much.

He turned and looked at me. His eyes flared, then went stone-cold. "You're lying," he said. "Don't fucking lie to me. I'm going to find out what really happened tonight, one way or another. I'd like to hear it from you."

We drove home in silence. I went straight into the bedroom, and Alex followed me. All I wanted to do was go to sleep. I was about to unzip my skirt when I remembered the bruises on my hip. I sat down on the edge of the bed, apologized over and over, begged Alex to let me sleep. I swore that I'd tell him everything when I woke up. We heard the television go on in the den. Kevin and Marisol were awake. Alex went downstairs and told them to get dressed. The three of them left together. I crawled under the covers and went to sleep.

39

When I woke up it was just starting to get dark outside. Alex's wedding ring was on the night table. When had he taken it off? He must have come home while I was asleep and deposited his ring there for me to find. Hung over, shaky, ashamed, I looked at my two summonses—driving while intoxicated, blood alcohol .2, and possession of less than one quarter of a gram of a controlled substance, a disorderly person's offense. I couldn't believe what I'd done. I took a shower, paced, tried to eat, and called a couple of my sisters, but it was Saturday night and nobody was home.

When Alex came in he seemed more sad than angry. I waited until the kids had gone to bed, then told him where I'd been, more or less. I told him I *had* gone to a bar with some women from my office. We met a man there who sold us the cocaine. I told him I'd gone out into the parking lot to do a line with this guy and he'd attacked me. I opened my robe, showed him. The color went out of Alex's face. He pushed the robe off my shoulders, let it drop to the floor, ran his fingers over my hip and thigh.

"Rita, were you raped?" He spoke so slowly.

"No, I wasn't. I screamed and two young guys came running out from the bar."

I expected an explosion. Fury would have been easier to take. I've never seen Alex look so befuddled. I was injured and his impulse was to nurse me, but he was repulsed by me at the same time. In his face I could see the opposing forces at work. He stood perfectly still for a moment, his hand over his mouth.

"You're not telling me the whole story," he said.

"I told you, Alex. I got drunk. I met this guy, he had cocaine, he tried to rape me. That's what happened, Alex."

"If you all bought the cocaine together, why were you alone with this son of a bitch in the parking lot?"

I didn't answer him.

SPLIT SKIRT

"You know what I think really happened? You were out in the parking lot fooling around, and things got out of hand. He wanted to fuck you, and you wouldn't let him. Is that what happened, Rita?"

I nodded my head.

"I've had it, Rita. Do you understand me? For months you've been walking around here like you'd rather be someplace else. You're so miserable? You don't want to be here anymore? Go. Get out. I have had it."

I didn't go, obviously. Since that night we've barely spoken. We sleep in one bed but don't touch. Alex leaves early in the morning, and I don't see him until ten or eleven at night. I'm afraid to have it out with him because I know when I do he's going to tell me he wants a divorce. I'll bet you anything he's already seen a lawyer. I'm so afraid he's spending time with his ex-wife. Lee's calling the house a lot more than she used to. When she came to pick up the kids last Saturday, she was wearing this cute little white dress, and Alex carried Marisol's bag out to the car, and they stood and talked for twenty minutes in the street. I couldn't see Alex's face, but Lee was smiling an awful lot. I watched from an upstairs window.

Last night he stayed out until two, and when he got into bed, I could feel guilt coming off him in waves. He's waiting until all of this is over to tell me, I know it. He was afraid I'd have a complete breakdown if I had to face going to jail and losing him at the same time.

Alex and Lee are going to get back together, pick up where they left off. Where does that leave me? I become just an unfortunate chapter in their family history. I'm the woman Alex killed time with until Lee decided she wanted him back.

SIX

"Alex is *your* husband now, Rita," I say. "Don't forget that. Try not to jump to conclusions. Wait until you get out of here and can find out exactly what's going on. You'll drive yourself crazy imagining things."

Rita nods at me, looks down into her lap. She's all talked out. Poor thing, she's exhausted. She rubs her face with both hands, licks her lips, and looks over at the clock on the wall.

It's almost three now, which means my husband's plane has just landed; his driver is watching for him in the terminal. John will go into the office, have dinner out, if he eats at all, come home to an empty house.

When I told John I didn't want him trying to get my sentence changed, he was baffled at first, then furious. My kleptomania has caused so much disruption in our lives; to him it must have

43

seemed I was raising the stakes by insisting on going to jail. He agreed to stay out of it finally because he didn't know what else to do. Over the years he's tried rage and compassion, he's forbidden me to step foot inside a store, sent me to half a dozen doctors, encouraged me to sign up for college. He went so far as to applaud my interest in genealogy. For my birthday he sent me to Ireland with an expert from New York and a tour group of other rich women so I could discover my roots. I stole a lace tablecloth from a department store in Dublin.

"Marriage is stronger than you know, Rita," I say. "When I look back, I can't believe some of the hits my marriage has survived."

"What I'm afraid of, Mrs. Tyler, is that I'm going to be one of the hits Alex's marriage to Lee survives."

She turns away, pulls the rubber band out of her hair, loops it over index finger and thumb, stretches it. She takes aim at a cigarette butt on the floor, then a crumpled tissue, then the leg of a nearby chair. She shoots, and the rubber band sails through the air. She gets up to retrieve it.

I'm old enough to be her mother, but it's hard to feel maternal toward Rita. I don't think I'd want her as a daughter. She's too mangy or fierce or stunted or something. Something. I'll bet Rita was something when she was a girl. With those long, straight limbs, those clear eyes. I imagine that she negotiated with the world in good faith then, that her current flowed along healthy fibers. Now it misfires, sparks, smokes.

I wonder about her background. Is Rita the daughter of blue-collar parents who struggled to send her to college, or was her father a doctor or a lawyer and she slipped? She's earthy like a barmaid, sits with her legs spread. Daughters in my town sometimes affect this kind of crudeness. They use foul language, marry mechanics, live only to see their mothers blanch.

SPLIT SKIRT

. . .

Dinner is exactly the same as lunch—meat loaf. I offer Rita my ketchup packet, but she shakes her head no. We eat in silence. The other women are quieter than they were earlier; the long day is taking its toll.

A buzzer sounds. We line up and are led down a hallway, through a pair of double doors, outside. The yard is large, the fence chain-link. A coil of razor wire runs along the top. Women mill around, light cigarettes, lift their faces to the six o'clock sun.

Rita and I walk the perimeter, slowly, our heads down, our hands in our pockets. We pass a metal sign that warns us against communicating with anybody on the other side of the fence. It has the look and lettering of a No Parking sign. A woman with filthy blond hair sits on the ground, talking softly to herself and banging her forehead against her knees.

Ten o'clock is lights out. We take off our shoes in the dark and lie down. Outside a car door slams, a police radio squawks. Rita is fidgeting like a drug addict in the beginning of cold turkey— she may well be one, for all I know, alcohol, cocaine, marijuana. Rita's all the time wanting. Was I ever that way? I think so. I can remember a time when I was filled with righteous indignation. It lasted about a week and a half, as I recall. Rita would never believe it. She thinks she invented anger with unknown origins, mysterious rage.

A guard walks by, slapping her billy club against her palm and whistling.

Rita bolts upright. "It's no use," she says. "I can't sleep here. Can you?"

"You haven't given yourself much of a chance, Rita. Why don't you lie down and try to relax?"

She shakes her head, stands up, walks over to the bars, and looks out.

"How old are you, Mrs. Tyler?"

"Fifty-two."

"And you've been married thirty-four years?"

"That's right."

"Was John your high school sweetheart?"

"Not exactly," I say. "No."

SEVEN

I grew up in Atlantic City, Rita. My family didn't have any money. We lived hand-to-mouth. When I was sixteen, my mother saw an ad in the newspaper saying one of the big hotels on the boardwalk was hiring. She and I went down together. The manager of the coffee shop hired me on the spot, thanked my mother for coming, said he'd keep her application on file. I knew he didn't hire her because she was old and tired. I wondered if she knew.

As soon as school let out, I went to work and was absolutely wide-eyed. The hotel guests wore such beautiful clothes, ate fancy food at every meal. Some families stayed the entire summer, the fathers coming in on Friday nights from New York or Philadelphia. You cannot imagine how impressed I was by the splendor of the hotel itself and by the elegance of the people who stayed there. For the first time in my life, I understood how poor I was.

The work was hard. A hotel kitchen is a wild place. Cooks screamed at waitresses. The chef threw saucers and silverware. I learned to carry a tray on my shoulder and make coffee in a giant urn.

I worked in the coffee shop through the first summer. In September when the staff was cut, I was kept on in the formal dining room. I was being trained, taught how to serve so I'd be ready for the next season.

I met Vincent in December. He was a restaurant-supply salesman who came to Atlantic City twice a month. He had olive skin and jet-black hair. He'd be handsome if he weren't so dark, I said to myself when I first noticed him. He wasn't tall, five six or seven and slight—skinny, really, like Frank Sinatra in those days. A good dresser, stylish but not fussy.

He used to sit alone at a table for four, doing paperwork. In the wintertime prices were lowered, and salesmen could afford to eat in the dining room. He didn't flirt with me. He was serious, businesslike.

I had absolutely no experience with men. My love life up until then consisted of fantasies about one of my girlfriend's older brothers. He kept to himself, this fellow. He'd been to Korea and back again. I used to imagine we had a great secret love that would one day reveal itself. I hadn't been out on a single date, hadn't been kissed, and all of a sudden, along comes Vincent. This grown man who never smiled was watching me work.

One night Vincent came in just as we were closing the dining room. He asked me if he could talk to me when I was finished, then stood waiting in the lobby. I was carrying my coat when I walked out. He took it out of my hands and held it for me to put on. I'd seen men do that in the hotel, but nobody had ever done it for me.

We went for a walk. It was February, and the wind was fierce on the boardwalk. I had a scarf in my pocket but didn't want to put it on because I thought it made me look plain, like an immigrant woman. The wind and the ocean spray were too much finally, and I pulled out the scarf. As I was tying it, Vincent put his hands on my cheeks. "I could look at your face for hours," he said.

I knew I was taking a chance staying out after work. If my mother got home before I did, I'd catch hell, but I didn't care, so long as I could keep walking and holding Vincent's hand. We both had gloves on. Every so often he'd squeeze hard. I still remember the feel of his strong fingers through leather and wool.

Just as we turned to head back, he pulled me toward him and kissed me. Rita, it was some kiss. Boy oh boy, do I remember it—his lips opening against mine, his cheeks and nose and chin. The stirring I felt, the heat in the midst of cold air. I'd never been touched before. I swooned, and Vincent smiled and steadied me.

In his car in front of my apartment he told me he was leaving early the next morning but would be back in two weeks. He gave me fifty dollars, five ten-dollar bills, and told me to buy myself a dress so he could take me out when he got back. Fifty dollars! I held the money in my hand all the way upstairs.

The apartment was dark and quiet. Everybody was asleep. My mother would never expect me to come home late, so she didn't worry, I realized. My four brothers slept in the living room then because our apartment only had two bedrooms. My sister Margie and I in one, my mother and father in the other. The boys stretched out on the couch and chairs. My youngest brother, James, was sleeping on the floor, curled up on a blanket like a dog. I stepped over him, shuddered to think what Vincent would say if he saw how we lived.

I washed up, put on my nightgown, and slipped into bed beside Margie. The room was stifling. Margie used to get colds all the time, so my mother would keep the heat up. What torture it was, lying still in that stuffy room when what I wanted to do was get up and start the next day so the two-week wait would be that much shorter.

I held on to the thrill for the next few days—I'd kissed an older man on the boardwalk!—but as time went on, I began to get scared. What if Vincent didn't show up on the day he said he would? What if he never came back? I told myself I'd be okay. At least I'd been kissed. Plus I had the money. Fifty dollars out of the blue was just plain good.

To keep my spirits up I made a big project of buying the dress. I watched women getting in and out of cabs, went to the movies just to see what the actresses wore, studied customers in the dining room. What sort of dress was appropriate for dinner out with a man who wore suits and ties every day? I'll say this for myself: I knew how much I didn't know.

In the lobby of the hotel I saw a notice that Best, a New York department store, was having a road show at Spray Beach, another big hotel. In those days some of the top stores would go around the country selling their merchandise out of hotel suites. I knew I'd find what I wanted there.

I wore my good dress, was shaking as I walked in. A smart-looking saleswoman came right up to me, and I told her I was going to a dance in Philadelphia—I thought that would send the right message. She didn't ask me another thing about it, went right to work flipping through the racks. She chose a pale-blue satin dress that was cinched at the waist; she said it flattered my figure without being too revealing and brought out my beautiful eyes. It cost thirty-nine dollars, which didn't leave much for shoes or stockings, but I was happy to spend some of my own money for the rest.

Hiding my dress from my family was a problem. How could I get it upstairs without crumpling it? I knew I wouldn't be able to press it, so it was important that it not get wrinkled. I skipped school, picked up the dress, walked upstairs with it perfectly brazenly, as if I did that sort of thing all the time. Nobody was home. I got even bolder and put the dress on, then I walked through the apartment in it, sat on the arm of the couch and crossed my legs, pretended I was flitting around at a cocktail party.

The door swung open, and in walked my father, drunk. He tended bar when he was working at all, but some days he'd get too drunk to work and be sent home. There we were, the two of us trapped like rats. He was drunk in the middle of the day, and I was perched on the couch in a blue satin dress. Neither of us said a word. He shook his head, sneered, and lurched off to his room. I waited for a few minutes, then hid the dress in the back of my closet, put my raincoat on the hanger over it. When I saw my father later that night, I was terrified, waiting for him to explode. He didn't. He lowered his eyes, hung over and sheepish. He didn't remember seeing me.

Vincent came back on the day he said he would. When I first saw him, my heart sank. I'd built him up so much during the two weeks that when he walked in he looked puny, not dashing the way I remembered him. But that passed. He looked at me with those dark eyes, helped me on with my coat, offered his arm, and I was flying.

He wasn't staying at the Andover, he told me, because he didn't want to make trouble. He thought my boss might not approve of my dating a customer. Such a thing had never occurred to me. I imagined Vincent up in New York selling his restaurant supplies and thinking about me and my boss. It was the first taste I'd ever had of being taken care of, and it felt damn good.

We went for a drive. The weather was bad, sleeting and raw. His car was clean and warm and smelled of spearmint gum. He told me he'd thought about me whenever he was alone, counted the days until he'd see me again. He didn't gush; his words were clipped. I believed Vincent and I were outsiders, people the world didn't necessarily open its arms to.

We went back to his room at the Sandpiper. I knew I was committing a crime every step of the way. Not a crime—a sin. The hotel rooms of men were more than off-limits, they were like outer space, they barely existed, but I wanted to go. With his hand on my elbow, he steered me past the front desk and onto the elevator. In his room he poured two drinks from a bottle of Dewars, told me to sip mine slowly. The scotch made me gag. Through sheer force of will I got it down, my very first drink. It warmed my insides and went right to my head. Vincent was sitting on the bed. I got up from my chair, walked over, and sat down beside him.

He turned off the light and undressed me. He unhooked my garters and took off my stockings more carefully than I ever had, then stood and undressed himself. I wanted to watch but was embarrassed and lowered my eyes.

For a moment we lay side-by-side without touching, and then he kissed me. He was gentle at first, his touch slow and deliberate, but then it seemed he couldn't restrain himself any longer, and I was grateful. I wanted to see Vincent lose control over me.

When he got up to get a condom out of his suitcase and then sat down to put it on, I took a good look at his penis. It wasn't the first one I'd seen. My younger brothers had them, of course.

SPLIT SKIRT

I'd always thought theirs looked like internal organs covered with skin. I'd never seen one erect before, and didn't care for it, this thing protruding beneath his belly. It looked like an anatomical distortion to me, a deformity, or like something he might strap on from time to time for a specific purpose, like fins on a diver's feet. I didn't understand how in the world he could walk around with that all the time.

It hurt, really hurt. If I'd had the nerve, I would have made him stop. Oh, my God, it seemed to go on forever. When it was finally over, Vincent settled down, held me tight, and said he'd been looking for so long.

When I got home that night, I locked myself in the bathroom and cried my eyes out. Something important had finally happened to me. I'd been naked with a man, and he'd touched me everywhere, places inside me I'd never touch myself. There was a smell unlike any other between my legs, and I was tender there, sore. I'd done it. I knew what it was.

The next night he took me out to dinner at Zaberers, the best restaurant in Atlantic City back then. I looked beautiful in my blue dress, had my first martini, felt what it was to be a woman in relation to a man. Vincent was handsome and graceful. I didn't stiffen when he touched me, didn't worry about what I said or didn't say.

We went back to his room right after dinner, and Rita, we couldn't stop. A few times we thought we were finished and would start to dress, tell each other we had to get me home, then end up back in bed. I had an orgasm before I knew what one was. I felt it starting to happen, closed my eyes, opened my mouth, screamed. When I came back to earth, Vincent was gazing at me like I was a miracle.

From then on he came to Atlantic City every two weeks. I lived a double life and loved it. Most days I did the ordinary things—

helped my mother, went to school, worked at the hotel—but for a day or two every couple of weeks I was a woman with a lover. I'd be so full of myself while I lounged on Vincent's bed in the afternoon or blithely took a bath while he shaved.

Every so often I'd be shaken by the thought that I'd gone all the way with a man. I knew I should feel guilty, so I tried to. I'd lost my virginity before marriage; what would that mean for my future? I don't think I ever believed I'd go the ordinary route. My sister, Margie, went steady with boys from school. She wore their I.D. bracelets, came home from the boardwalk with stuffed animals and pinwheels they'd won for her. It simply wasn't like that for me. At the hotel I'd occasionally see women by themselves, women in their thirties and forties who took vacations alone. They paid their own bills, sat by themselves on the beach. I identified with those women and not sadly. I believed that's how I would live. The women who came with husbands and children reminded me of my mother despite their fancy clothes and polished fingernails. They argued with eight-year-olds, policed their husbands' drinking at dinner.

God, how I used to think about Vincent when he was away. I'd get a few good memories every time he was in town, his profile so handsome in the dim light, the way he stared at himself in the mirror while he tied his tie. I'd savor them, use them to keep myself going.

While all of this was happening, Margie was fighting with my mother over a boyfriend. My mother thought this fellow was too old for Margie. A college boy, he might have been twenty. He'd come over, bring Margie flowers and cheap little toys. Once he brought a puppet, and all evening he had the puppet tell Margie how pretty she was. Even Margie was embarrassed by that; she giggled nervously and wouldn't look at me. My mother refused to let Margie go out on dates with this boy. She was only allowed to see him at our house. What a stink! Margie stormed around, treated my mother very badly. All of this commotion about a boy with a puppet, when I was slipping off to a man's hotel room right under my mother's nose.

One morning my mother got me out of bed to give my youngest brother a bath. I'd been out with Vincent the night before, had gotten in very late and hadn't dared go into the bathroom to wash for fear of waking my mother. Kneeling by the bathtub, I could smell Vincent on me. I pulled the front of my nightgown away from my body, stuck my nose inside, closed my eyes and breathed deep. When I looked up, my mother was standing over me, her eyes flinty. I was sure she could smell me, thought she was going to smack me. I struggled to get to my feet. She threw a towel in my face and said, "Get the baby dressed."

I didn't keep track of my periods—I'd never had a reason to— but gradually I began to feel it had been too long since I'd had one. I didn't panic. It was a constant low-level worry that I fully expected to take care of itself. Then I started getting tired like I'd never been before. I could barely get through the day. One afternoon I fell sound asleep in English class. There was a tremendous pull downward, so that if I was standing, I wanted to sit, if I was sitting, I wanted to lie down, and if I was lying down, I wanted to sleep.

I knew what was happening by then but couldn't bring myself to name it or tell Vincent. The next time he was in town, going to bed with him was like getting assaulted. I lay under him, praying he'd finish fast.

I started getting hungry then, was starving all the time. At work I'd talk the chef into making me sandwiches from leftover prime rib. I craved the fat, oily and brown. At home I'd sneak food because I was afraid my mother would notice my appetite. After school I'd buy packages of butterscotch Tastycakes and eat them one after the other as I walked down the street.

I told Vincent the next time I saw him, waited until our clothes were off and we were in bed. He sat straight up. How could I be pregnant? He was careful, always used protection. Maybe the baby wasn't his. It had certainly been easy enough for him to get me into bed. How did he know what I did when he wasn't around? "I can't marry you, if that's what you're thinking," he said, pulling the sheet off and putting both feet on the floor. "I'm already married."

The instant he said it I realized I'd known all along. I had tried to convince myself that Vincent's life was what he said it was, going from one hotel to another, then back to a small apartment in north Jersey, but naïve as I was, I knew no grown person's life is that simple. I would have continued to see him even if I found out he was lying, so what was the point of pressing?

He said he knew a woman who knew a doctor. He got up and dialed the hotel operator. While he talked I got dressed, then sat on the edge of the bed. I'd put on weight already; my face and breasts and ankles were bloated. I felt vulgar, low-class, fat.

The abortion was done in a doctor's office after hours. Vincent handed over a stack of twenty-dollar bills, and the doctor counted them twice. He was young and mild-mannered. He gave me ether and held my hand as I went under. When I woke up there was a pad between my legs, warm and wet. I smelled blood and threw up in a metal basin. The doctor made me put on my clothes right away, even though I could barely stand up.

Vincent ministered to me tenderly on the way home, kept putting his hand on my forehead to see if I had a fever. I didn't say one word until he stopped the car outside my building. I turned, looked at him, and felt rage so powerful it was all I could do to keep from hitting him. I wanted revenge, wanted to hurt him, to say something that would spark shame and guilt. "Do you have children?" I asked.

There was more life in his eyes than I'd ever seen before. "Three," he said. "Two girls and a boy."

I listened to him cry without so much as looking over at him. His sobs didn't move me any more than the sound of cars passing on the street. One noise, another—what difference did it make? I kept my eyes on the door to my building.

The next day I couldn't get up for school. I told my mother I was sick with my period, and for once she believed me. I must have looked a wreck. All day I lay in bed nursing a sadness like nothing I'd ever known before. Something had been taken from me. No, I'd handed it over. Not a baby, exactly. My self. The person I'd been before. I knew from then on I'd have to include the abortion in my understanding of who I was. No matter what else ever happened to me in my life, there it would be.

EIGHT

I had one too, Mrs. Tyler.

I was twenty and screwing a much older man. I met him in a bar and went after him knowing all the while he was a lowlife. He was handsome in a dissolute sort of way; he could have been Tom Selleck's alcoholic older brother. He was separated from his third wife and had an apartment in a high-rise building, a bona fide bachelor pad. We didn't go on dates. He never took me out to dinner or anything close. We would make vague plans to be at the same bar, and sometimes he'd show up. His bed was enormous—super king-size mattress, extra-long pillows. There were stacks and stacks of bills on his kitchen table and pictures of his many children from his three marriages propped up on counters and held with magnets to the refrigerator; wallet-size shots would be stuck in the frames of eight-by-tens.

I remember being in his apartment one morning after he left for work. I wanted to leave him a sexy little note, since I'd pretended to be asleep when he left. There was a memo pad with "From the Desk of the Big Cheese" printed on it. I wrote one note and didn't like it, wrote another and another and another. Pretty soon I'd used up half the pad and still didn't have a version that satisfied me. I stuffed all the rejects in my pockets and got out of there. At home I balled up the crumpled papers and pushed them deep into the kitchen garbage, disgusted by my own tentativeness.

I felt outclassed by him in bed. He expected me to, I don't know, tear him up, and the only sex I'd known until then had been tame, sincere and gropy. He'd watched too many porno movies, fucked too many women. With me he always seemed like he was waiting for the good stuff to start. He'd look vaguely exasperated. I remember having sex with him on his black sectional couch, me on top. I didn't have any idea how to do what I was doing, couldn't get the hang of it. He kept saying, "It's *your* cock, it's *your* cock," which gave me no direction whatsoever.

From this idiot I got pregnant. I was on the Pill but didn't like taking it. I was convinced it made me hyperactive and overly emotional. My heart would race for no reason at all, and I'd get teary if anybody looked at me funny, so I'd skip a day, take two pills the next day, that sort of thing. I was waitressing at night, and just like you, I started getting tired. I worked until two. By about nine o'clock I'd be moving slowly, telling myself if I just kept going, the night would eventually end.

I went to Planned Parenthood for the test. The woman who told me I was pregnant wanted to counsel me right then, but I wouldn't let her. I had to get out of there. I promised I'd come back in a day or two and went to the supermarket, of all places. I tore up and down the aisles, terrified, half out of my mind. I think I went there because it was the most ordinary place. The aberration that had introduced itself into my life would be most vivid to me there. And it was. In the Shop-Rite I was somebody new.

I never told the father. Our paltry relationship went on as it had. The night before my abortion I had sex with him. I'm not sure what I was about then. I wanted very much to be unconventional, tough. I hated the way so many girls acted soft, like suckers, because I knew that wasn't genuine. Growing up with seven sisters, I understood better than most that girls are not weaker than boys, or more pliant or sweeter or less ruthless. I'd lived every single day of my life with brainy, ferocious, willful girls. I was completely unprepared to pretend I was gentle by nature. I overcompensated, though, acted hard like a thug of a boy. I was as far from my authentic self as the most simpering girl.

My sister Eva, my big sister, took me for the abortion. When I'm having a bad time, Eva gets a look in her eyes that says, "Ri, somebody giving you trouble here?" We drove to the clinic in her beat-up old car, and I felt safe, didn't care if I ever found a boyfriend, a man of my own. Eva and I would just cruise along together, having our wild nights and our long, laughing talks. When something awful happened, like this, we'd go through it together.

At the clinic five other women and I were led into a small room for a counseling session. The woman in charge assumed we all had boyfriends or husbands, anguished men hovering in the background. She told us to let our partners take care of us. We would get through this together, she said. It was 1986, for Christ's sake. Hadn't she ever heard of a one-night stand? Her assumption ignited the shame in me, the slutty feeling I wanted so much to rise above but couldn't, finally. I did the worst thing I could possibly have done: I played along, pretended there was some worried boy waiting for me.

One woman said her husband was impatient with her. "Enough crying already," he told her. "It's like having a tooth pulled."

I was sent to a cubicle to undress and put on a hospital gown. I have never been so scared. My feet and hands were freezing, and sweat streamed down from my armpits. I was panting. If I get any more nervous, I thought, I'll lose my mind. Just before they did it, they gave me a shot of Demerol, and everything eased. The drug gave me back to myself for a few seconds.

I don't remember much about the abortion itself. There was a doctor and a nurse and the usual stirrups and my bare ass sticking to the paper lining over vinyl. The pain made me imagine there was a wire deep inside me, like a string on a bow, made of nerve tissue, being plucked over and over again.

When I walked out to the waiting room, Eva got to her feet. She stood so close to me while we paid the bill that our hips touched. We'd come up with the money between us, put off paying our rent. She put her arm around me while we walked to the car. We drove home slowly, then she made me a turkey sandwich but didn't nag me to eat it.

What happened to me then is just what happened to you. I was overcome with sadness. I fell apart. Eva sat with me until I could sleep.

For weeks afterward the little pinprick where the Demerol had gone in remained visible on the top of my hand. I used to rub it, hold it against my tongue. I didn't want to forget any of it. I was convinced that if I did, if my memories of the shock and fear and shame I'd experienced faded, I'd be lost to myself for good. That

little red mark on the top of my hand became my connection to the truth.

That was seven years ago, but even now, when I cry hard, when I really let loose over anything, I find myself thinking and sometimes even saying oh, my baby, oh, my baby boy. I'm not sure when I came to believe the baby would have been a boy. It's something I know but don't understand. Intuition tells me it's so.

NINE

*M*rs. Tyler is still sleeping, but I've been awake for fifteen or twenty minutes, lying here almost without words, a receptor for the sensations of waking up in jail. Time spirals. The air is dense like on a cool, cloudy day. Moving against it, rolling onto my side or bringing my knees up, is hard like pushing through water.

I hear people working in the kitchen, calling out to each other, pushing carts with squeaky wheels. I feel inert and, strangely, cared for. When I wake up at home I reach for Alex, find him with my hand or knee. He eases toward me while I review what I have to do that particular morning, afternoon, and evening. Here I can be perfectly passive. The day will come and get me.

Alex and I don't wake up that way anymore. How long has it been? Weeks. Months.

Agnes Rossi

I feel longing, sweet and serious, psychic groping in the dark—for the expanse of Alex's back, the hair at his temples soft and warm from sleep. Is he right now opening his eyes and patting my side of the bed? If we could hold on to that impulse toward each other, literally toward each other across six inches of mattress, we'd do so much better.

A guard comes past, clapping her hands and calling out, "Get up, let's go, now." She takes pleasure in shouting, this one. There are two types: those who suspend judgment and those who consider themselves part of the punishment.

Mrs. Tyler is groggy and looks like hell. Her hair is mashed and sparse in the shadowy light. She sits on the edge of her bed for a moment, then digs through her bag for soap, toothpaste, toothbrush.

There's a distinct awkwardness between us. What in the world made us talk so much last night? I'm embarrassed now, wish I'd kept my mouth shut. I can't ever tell anybody anything important without some part of me wishing I hadn't.

We wash and use the toilet. The dim light and our wariness help. We don't speak or make eye contact. We breathe through our mouths. I change my underwear and shirt. When I've worn everything I've got in my knapsack, it will be time to go home.

Mrs. Tyler uses a pink rat-tail comb to repair her hairstyle. No mirror here, and still she teases one section at a time expertly. She grimaces as she sprays the dome with White Rain. Standing near the bars to escape the fumes, I wonder how come she's allowed to have hair spray here. Couldn't the can be used as a weapon? Couldn't she conk somebody on the head with that?

Breakfast is oatmeal, exactly what I'd be having at home. It's good and thick, the milk is cold. The coffee's a disappointment—

no kick. I think of the coffee maker on my kitchen counter at home, steaming cheerfully, doing its part. Alex must be making Kevin and Marisol's lunches, a job I usually do and like. I was surprised to find I enjoy the most mundane duties of parenting— washing and folding their downsized clothes, lugging home glass jugs of apple juice, waiting for Kevin and Marisol in the dentist's office, then listening to reports on their teeth.

After breakfast we're sent out to the yard, but it starts to drizzle and we gather by the door. The guards are busy. There seems to be a logistical problem of some kind. Oh, I see—the men are in the dayroom. Where can they put us? It's raining hard now, and the women are grumbling. "This ain't right," somebody shouts from the rear. "Chill," a guard says under her breath.

We're corralled in the hallway. The men are paraded past us, hundreds of them. What a thing! Men and women wave and stand on tiptoes and make lewd kissing sounds. Hey, baby, both ways. Everybody is grinning, even the guards. It feels like a lucky break. Boys and girls. Them and us. Hellooooooooo, Betty.

Spirits are high as we head into the dayroom. Women stretch and smile, shake out the fronts of damp T-shirts. I hurry to get a good place on line for the phone.

When I dial home, the phone rings four times and then there's a series of clunks; the receiver must have slipped and hit the counter, then the floor. "Hello," Marisol says finally. The operator asks if she'll accept the charges for a collect call, and I coach her. "Say yes, sweetie." The operator asks Marisol if her mother is home, and Marisol, confused by the two voices, gets flustered and says hello again.

"Put Daddy on," I say.

"Daddy's not here."

The operator breaks in and says I'll have to call back. Only an adult can accept charges. The operator apologizes and hangs up. I try to dial again, but the guard catches me, takes the receiver right out of my hand, says one call to a customer.

I wonder why Marisol isn't in school until I remember it's Saturday morning. Of course. Alex dropped me off here yesterday, Friday, a little over twenty-four hours ago. So where is he now? Has he just run out for milk, or is he gone for the day? I look around at the guards and the locked doors. I want only to get out of here and go home.

Mrs. Tyler is sitting on the floor in the corner with her back against the wall, even though there are dozens of empty chairs. I like her for that. I slide down the opposite wall so that we're knee-to-knee.

"Alex isn't home. My stepdaughter answered the phone, and she didn't know how to accept a collect call. The operator cut us off." Telling Mrs. Tyler what happened defuses it, puts it in perspective. Some of the urgency gets spent in saying the words. Encouraged and wanting more of the same, I go on. "I can't believe Alex didn't wait for my call."

"Did you think he would?"

So much for lightening my load.

"Did I think he would? Yes. Isn't he worried about me? If he were in jail, I'd worry about him."

"Give the man some room, for God's sake. If you were smart, Rita, you wouldn't call him again."

"I know. But I can't do that. This place is too weird. Talking to Alex will help keep me together here. And all of a sudden I have to know what's going on with him. How come you haven't called home yet?"

"Because it would be humiliating for my husband, and for me. John doesn't need to talk to me from jail."

"I think that's sad."

SPLIT SKIRT

"I knew you would."

There isn't another inmate within twenty feet of us. The other women are clustered around the phones or the TV. I look over at Mrs. Tyler, imagine her standing at a glass display case in Bloomingdale's, cupping a lipstick in her hand, shooting it up her sleeve with her middle finger.

Mrs. Tyler opens her suitcase and takes out a crossword-puzzle magazine and a yellow pencil. I want to read but wind up passing *Wuthering Heights* back and forth between my hands, thumbing its pages.

I feel peculiar, as if I'd had a drink or taken one hit of a joint. The air in here feels so close, the scratch of Mrs. Tyler's pencil inordinately loud. When I close my eyes, her face takes ten or fifteen seconds to fade out.

The buzzer sounds. It's lunchtime. Didn't we just get back from breakfast? We join the stream of women heading to the cafeteria. I bite the inside of my cheek, rub my face, try to clear my head.

Macaroni and cheese, smooth and soft. Too-sweet orange drink. A walkie-talkie bleats in the hand of a guard. At least a dozen roaches scurry up and down the wall behind Mrs. Tyler. I put my hand on her arm and look toward them. She gets up and comes around to sit beside me.

Out in the yard I tell Mrs. Tyler to take her laps without me. She looks disappointed, but I don't care. I crave privacy. I'm sure if I could be alone for just a few minutes, I could shake this spacy feeling.

I want to sit still, so I have to go to the center of the yard. The edges are active. Women walk there. In the middle people sit and talk or stare out at the street. I pick a spot as far from the others as I can get. Mrs. Tyler passes, smiles, hopes I'll change my mind and join her. I put my head on my knees, close my eyes.

Traffic sounds, women's voices, the smell of my own body after a tense day and night without a shower. I take a deep breath and begin to calculate how many hours are left, but lose my way in the numbers. The sun is out now. It's warm on my scalp, on the part in my hair.

I get up and walk over to the farthest corner of the fence. From here I can see the back of the jail, the old brick section. Engraved in the stone above one of the doors is the word *Women.* The letters are worn; I have to look closely to make them out.

Women.

Women's department, I think.

Before he retired, my father was a newspaperman, an editor at the New York *Daily News.* Every once in a while my mother would take all of us girls to see him at work. We'd tromp through the newsroom, buy sodas from the machines, read the comics in the next day's paper.

My sisters and I used to play newspaper at home. End tables, the coffee table, the kitchen table—every available flat surface would become a desk. We'd scribble on copy paper my father brought home for us, call each other on imaginary phones, use my mother's scissors to cut up her magazines. When people asked me what I wanted to be when I grew up, I'd say a newspaper lady, which is what my mother had been when she met and married my father.

I remember one particular trip to the *News.* It was late, ten or eleven at night. My mother had taken us to see *My Fair Lady* on Broadway. My father met us in the lobby. On our way to the newsroom, we passed a sign that said WOMEN'S DEPARTMENT. The lights were out there, the desks unoccupied. My father made a joke about it—"Women's Department," he said. "Closed down for the night, nothing doing."

My friends' fathers were all businessmen, nine-to-fivers. I thought it was cool that my father left for work at dinnertime. There was something selfless about his working all night so the world could have its newspaper first thing in the morning. When I got out of bed at six or six-thirty, the four-star edition of the *Daily News* would be on our kitchen table. Like the elves in *Pinocchio* who creep in at night and make shoes, my father made newspapers while we slept.

I remember standing in that hallway and looking at the dark, vacant Women's Department. I felt embarrassed—I didn't know quite why, until I decided that my father was right to make fun of women, to dismiss them. If women were too lazy to work on the newspaper at night, if they got up and went to work in the morning like everybody else, they deserved ridicule. We walked on to the newsroom.

Men with their shirtsleeves rolled up shouted at one another, walked quickly, slouched down in their chairs, smoked. They smiled at us almost shyly, kidded my father about all the weddings he'd have to pay for, said he should set up ladders outside each of our windows. A young man, a reporter, put his coat on as he hurried by us. "What's up?" my father called after him. "A fucking fire," the reporter said. My father winced. "Watch your mouth," he growled. "My girls." The reporter looked sheepish, apologized.

Walking us to the car, my father said he hoped none of us would go into the newspaper business when we grew up. The language, he said, the night hours. A newsroom is no place for a woman.

Pretty soon my sisters and I lost interest in playing newspaper.

Agnes Rossi

We switched to a boyfriend/girlfriend game wherein we took the names of some of the dolls that were marketed as Barbie's friends; our boyfriends were the four members of our favorite singing group, the Monkees. Any one of us could initiate a game simply by declaring who she was and which Monkee was hers. "Francie, Davy," one of us would shout, and the game would begin. Davy Jones was the cutest Monkee, plus he had a British accent, so he was always the first to go. "Micky, Tutti," the second sister would call. "Peter, Casey," was always third. The least desirable of the Monkees was Mike Nesmith, the one with the wool cap, the one who rarely smiled. We knew that he was married, in real life, to a woman named Phyllis. The slowest sister not only got stuck with Mike, she also had to be a wife instead of a fun-loving, free-agent girlfriend.

TEN

Mrs. Tyler stares at the food on her plate: a piece of fish, baked, brownish, canned peas the color of olives, a Dixie cup of applesauce. I'm afraid she's summoning hope in the form of appetite. If she says this looks good, if she says anything even vaguely cheerful, I'm getting up and moving to another table.

She's quiet, thank God, even cranky. We're capable of comfortable silence now. The fish is slippery, promising stomach cramps in the night, loose bowels. After a few bites we give up on it and eat our applesauce as if it's ice cream—cup in one hand, spoon in the other. We want to go home.

What's Alex doing right now? Is he attempting to cook dinner for Kevin and Marisol, or are they opening menus in a diner? I've been fantasizing about his coming and taking me out of here like

Richard Gere in *An Officer and a Gentleman.* White uniform, easy gait. Deborah Winger rescued from the drudgery of the assembly line, carried out like a bride over a threshold. I imagine Alex's long strides across the cafeteria floor, his sly smile that says he paid somebody off, called in a favor. "Let's go," he'll say, and I'll stand up. In the car I'll kiss kiss kiss him while he tries to tell me how he did it.

Nothing remotely like this has ever happened to me. I conjure it up with no difficulty at all.

Alex. How did things get so out of whack between us? When I get home I'll ask him to go into counseling with me. I'll tell him that I don't care what's happened between him and Lee. Please, Alex, I'll say. You and I will sit across the desk from a professional who will help us sort everything out.

Therapy, terrapin, turtle. People in therapy move slowly, weighed down. And the rest of us think well of them. The tortoise and the hare. Small wizened face, short legs for small steps.

The lines at the phones are long. Impatience flares under my skin, making the muscles in my legs twitch. I might not make it to the front; I might lose control. When I was a teenager, I worked in an ice cream parlor. Business was bad; an hour could go by without a single customer. I'd stand behind the counter, look at the tidy rows of sundae dishes and banana-split boats, the forlorn little pot of hot fudge, and wonder what would happen if I went berserk and started breaking glass, cleared whole shelves with my forearm. The owner would come running, of course, but would he call the police or my parents? Would I get taken out of there in handcuffs, or with my mother's arm around my shoulders?

In here people must crack all the time. I think of the woman screaming cocksucker yesterday.

This line is barely moving. Damn. I stare at the guard, an older woman with short gray hair, a beefy trunk, and skinny legs. Why isn't she monitoring how long people talk? She notices my stare and returns it, raising her eyebrows and sticking out her chin.

Three women on the phone, and at any given moment at least one is crying. They're talking to men and kids and mothers. Sobs, hands over eyes, high-pitched trilling. It's pathetic.

My turn. The phone is picked up on the first ring. One second I'm celebrating because I think Alex is there waiting for my call, and the next I'm realizing the voice accepting the charges is a woman's. A woman? Lee.

It's Lee.

I'm stunned but polite. We've spoken on the phone so many times, carefully, always, courteously. "Lee, it's Rita."

"Rita," she says, "hi."

"Get Alex."

"Now, Rita, calm down."

"Don't say another word to me, Lee. Put my husband on the phone."

Silence. I'm terrified that Lee is going to hang up and I won't be able to call back. I'll walk away knowing that Alex's ex-wife is in my house, period. I shout Alex's name into the receiver. The gray-haired guard looks, takes a step toward me.

"Hello," Alex says, and his voice is protective. He's protecting *her*. Already. The shift has happened; I'm on the outside. I don't suspect this, I know it. The information is in Alex's voice the way a smell is in a room.

"What's she doing there? Tell me right now."

"Rita, when you get home—"

I'm crying and shouting and shaking. "Get her out of there. Get her out of my house—"

Two guards come toward me. "Hang up the phone. Say good-bye."

I turn and curl around the receiver. I feel a hand on the back of my neck, squeezing hard, and I try to writhe out from under it, my arm is wrenched backward. There is pain, sharp and hot, real damage about to be done. Another guard, a big blond farm girl with pigtails, comes at me head-on. The burning in my shoulder is all I know, and I kick. My foot hits her knee. There is a second or two of sheer terror, then pigtails punches me in the stomach, her fist smashing in just below my breastbone. If I could breathe, I would puke. I'm doubled over, knocked to the ground. Then Mrs. Tyler is there, pushing her way in, saying, "Leave her alone. Enough, please, enough." She's in between me and pigtails, gets grabbed from behind. I'm dragged out into the hall, down two flights of stairs. I'm completely limp now, nothing but scared.

It's two women, one black and the blonde, big asses in tight pants, smacking me on the side of the head. My ear, my cheek, my mouth. Stupid cunt, big-shot bitch, not so tough now. I sob, gag, beg them to stop.

ELEVEN

I should have stayed out of it, I know. It was Rita's fight. I should have minded my own business, of course. But when that big blond monster punched Rita in the stomach, something inside me flared, and I wasn't afraid. No, I thought. No.

Where is Rita right now?

My neck hurts, my back and shoulders too. I can't sit still. There must be some way for me to find out if Rita's all right.

I pull the brown pants out of my bag. I use my teeth to bite through the thread that runs along the waistband, then pull the stitches out with my fingers. I stack the five bills one on top of the other, flatten them out, fold them, and put them in my bra. After a moment I take them back out again, put two in one shoe, one in the other, the last two between my breasts.

I wasn't sure what good money would do me in jail. I figured I'd use it to ensure decent treatment but didn't know exactly how. I thought if another prisoner was harassing me, I might pay her to leave me alone. A guard might be bribed, made an ally.

These were the answers I gave my intellect when it wanted to know what my intuition was up to. A poor woman with a rich husband understands better than most that money protects.

I'm waiting to hear the footsteps of the night guard. Please let it be the same one as last night. While Rita slept I watched this guard, saw that she has no true investment in her job. The thick leather belt, the billy club, and the gun feel strange to her. She whistled the same tune over and over, self-consciously, the sort of whistle that suggests the whistler is uneasy doing what she's doing.

It's her. Thank God. Those same three notes are coming my way.

She's a black woman, thirty or so, tall and plain.

"Excuse me. Can I ask you something?"

Her eyes narrow. She's heard about Rita, is suspicious of me. "What?" she says, stopping reluctantly.

"My cellmate got in some trouble today, a fight in the day-room. She was taken out of there, and I haven't seen her since. Do you know how she is?"

"I know *where* she is. Downstairs. She'll be back up here in the morning and keep her damn mouth shut, do like she's told."

"I'll give you two hundred dollars if you take me to her."

"Yeah, right."

"I will. One hundred now and the other after I see her."

"You ain't got two hundred dollars."

"Yes, I do. I'll show it to you before we go anywhere."

I see what I'm praying for, a glint of greed in her eyes. She wants the money, is already thinking about how to spend it.

78

"No," she says. "It ain't worth it. Two hundred dollars, and if I get caught, I lose my job? No."

She's bargaining. I've got her. "Four hundred, then. Two now, two later. That's all I have."

She fakes skepticism. "Show me all four hundred."

"All right, but if you try to steal it from me, I'll scream bloody murder. I'm a rich woman. I'll see that you get fired if you try anything."

"Listen, bitch. You're asking me to do something, remember? Talking about rich and what you'll do when you get out. If you got so much pull, you wouldn't be in here yourself. I'll walk away right now, and then what? Why you want to see this one so bad? You queer?"

"I'm sorry, really. No, I'm married."

"Half of 'em is."

"I'm worried about her, that's all."

"Better worry about yourself."

"Are you interested or not?"

"I still ain't seen my money."

I take off my shoe, reach down into my bra, spread four bills across my palm, hand her two through the bars. She takes them.

"Okay, you listen to me now," the guard says, pushing the bills deep into her pants pocket. "I'm taking you to the infirmary because you got chest pains. You walk slow like you're sick, keep your eyes on the ground. If anybody comes up to us, you keep your mouth shut. Let me do the talking. You got that?"

I nod, and she puts her key in the lock.

The jail is quiet all around us, but electric, juicy. My heart's in my throat. People pass, and my guard says hey. The way is easy, smooth. Two long hallways, down some stairs. I'm high on my own daring.

The light in the basement is glaring, relentless. We stop at the foot of the stairs. "Wait here," the guard whispers. "Don't you move until I come back." She disappears around a corner. I hear footsteps, voices, the jangle of keys. A jail within a jail, this. I put my hand on my heart to steady myself.

The guard returns and motions for me to follow her. We pass a series of closed doors. She points at each one as we pass, counting. She stops, unlocks one, and pushes it open.

Rita's asleep, snoring softly on a cot, directly under a fluorescent light. I walk toward her, still exhilarated from the trip down. Then I see Rita's face.

Her bottom lip is split, and her cheek is so swollen that the hollow between her eye and nose is leveled. She looks deformed, like a Mongoloid version of herself.

All I can do is look at her.

Rita has intrigued and repulsed me from the moment I laid eyes on her. Standing here in this stinking place, I know why. For as long as I can remember I've been straining to put my finger on a word that means manipulated, distorted, deformed by harsh and unnatural forces—mangled, falsified, twisted, warped. None of these words has satisfied me. I've lived something that doesn't have a name. Right now, staring at Rita's face, I believe I have found my word. Rita. Snoring, dried blood on her lip, long legs bent at the knee, dirty feet, polished toenails. Here is my word.

"Rita," I whisper.

She goes on sleeping.

There's no sheet on the mattress, no pillow or blanket. She'll be stiff when she wakes up. She'll ache from the beating and the damp chill down here.

"Rita," I whisper again, put my hand on her shoulder.

She jumps up, covers her face with both hands, and shouts, "Get away from me, get away."

SPLIT SKIRT

"Shhhhhhhh, honey, it's me, Mrs. Tyler, see? It's okay, Rita, it's only me."

She settles down, starts to say something, stops, runs her fingers over her face.

Look at me, she's saying. Look what they did.

She feels smaller in my arms than I thought she would. Bony like my boys the last time they let me hold them. Okay, Rita, okay. Her sobs plow through her, through me, out.

TWELVE

*S*unday morning. The rug in the warden's office is pale blue, the desk is massive, the shades the good, heavy ones with circles at the ends of their pull strings. Mrs. Tyler and I sit on wooden chairs with corduroy cushions and wait. I was allowed to take a shower this morning, and I probed my fat lip and the swelling under my left eye with soapy fingers. Now, clean and aching, I welcome these gentle surroundings.

The warden makes an entrance like a doctor coming into an examining room. He's in his forties, meticulously groomed, wearing a good suit. His eyes are clear and intelligent. I expect sympathy from him, an apology even. I expect him to wince when he looks at my face.

"Ladies," he says and settles into his high-backed executive chair. He scans one piece of paper and then another, looks up at us. "Order must be maintained in a facility like this one. Without it, people get hurt. My job is all about order."

He looks at me. "You kicked a corrections officer, true?"

"My arm was wrenched behind—"

"Because you were told to hang up the phone and you refused." He turns to Mrs. Tyler, who wilts under his gaze. "And you took it upon yourself to interfere with officers trying to subdue an unruly inmate?"

I expect her to say they were using excessive force, she acted on impulse, something. She lowers her head.

"You are in jail, ladies. You are not at a fat farm or a resort. In jail you do exactly what you're told to do, or you pay the price. What I have here are indictments against you for assault. Formal charges will be filed. You're under arrest, ladies, all over again. I suggest you call your lawyers."

Back in our cell, Mrs. Tyler is furious. "I can't do it," she says. "I cannot go home and tell John I've been arrested again. He's going to kill me. I might as well not go home."

She doesn't care that she may end up back here; her husband's response is all that matters. She's frantic like a teenager who's cracked up the family car she didn't have permission to drive in the first place. Even her mannerisms are girlish. Her hands flutter around her face and neck, fuss with her clothes. She shakes her fingers as if she's got writer's cramp.

"You got me into this," she says. "I should have known better than to be friendly with somebody like you."

"What does that mean? Look, nobody told you to jump in. You did that on your own, and now you have to deal with the consequences. You, not your husband. He hasn't been charged with anything. Who knows, he might be enjoying his freedom.

Maybe he'll be glad to hear you have to come back for another couple days."

"Don't assume all men are like your husband. My John does not bring other women into our house. Nobody but me answers my phone."

"You don't know that."

"Yes, I do. How ugly of you to think that everybody's life is like yours. Your marriage is bad, so everybody's is? I'm sorry to disappoint you, Rita, but my marriage is sound."

"Really? Then why are you so terrified to call this wonderful husband of yours and tell him you did something stupid? You said he's going to kill you. Your words."

At the mention of her husband, Mrs. Tyler loses all interest in me. She sits down on her cot, puts her head in her hands. I don't matter here. All she knows is that her husband is going to be furious with her, disgusted by her. I am an annoyance, a momentary lapse in her otherwise good judgment.

"My life is a wreck and yours is not, huh?" I say. "Bullshit. You know why? Because you steal. You go into stores and take things without paying for them, and you can't stop yourself even when a judge tells you if you do it again, you're going to jail. You do it anyway."

She gets to her feet with murder in her eyes. She's going to hit me—Jesus Christ, will people stop hitting me?

She takes a deep breath, closes her eyes.

"Shut your mouth," she says. "You don't know anything about me."

Neither of us says another word. We lie on our sides, facing opposite walls. Before long a guard comes and gets Mrs. Tyler. Her lawyer is here to see her.

I'm alone. For the first time since the phone call, I face the knowledge that Lee is in my house. I know this: Alex and Lee are not irresponsible parents. A full-scale reconciliation must be under way, or they wouldn't be together in the presence of Kevin and Marisol.

The images start coming and won't stop. Alex and Lee falling back together, movements that were once familiar becoming familiar again. Their bodies know. The particular excitement of fucking somebody you used to fuck. The juice of somebody new without the awkwardness. In my bed?

Did they talk about me? *It was never right with Rita. Compared to how it is with you, I mean.*

Alex.

I'm being passed over. He's chosen her over me.

How long? Did it start after I got arrested or before? Back a couple of months ago when I was trying to make up with Alex, I kissed him deeply, ran my hand down his stomach and into his boxer shorts. I remember his lukewarm response.

What will happen now? What do I do? Throw him out, and Kevin and Marisol too? Will I live in our three-bedroom house by myself?

What did Alex hear yesterday when my arm was wrenched behind my back and I dropped the phone? The receiver must have hung there. I imagine Alex and Lee in my kitchen, the phone between them, listening, frowning, shaking their heads. *Poor Rita.*

THIRTEEN

"My lawyer thinks he can get them to drop the charges. And I spoke to him about you, Rita. You're tougher, he says, because you kicked the guard. But he's going to see what he can do."

The conciliatory tone in Mrs. Tyler's voice is more welcome than she knows. I can't fight the whole world at once.

"Thanks," I say. "How are you?"

"I'm okay," she says. "How are *you*?" Her gaze travels from the swelling below my eye to the split in my lip. "It won't be much longer now, Rita. Monday morning is less than twenty-four hours away."

Her voice has a tremor in it. For the first time I consider what this place, these days and nights, must be doing to her. The strip search, my beating, the language, even. She's here, though, in one piece. Meeting with her lawyer and counting the hours. Mrs. Tyler will get through whatever there is to be gotten through. To look at her rich-lady clothes and to know where she lives, you'd think all this would flatten her. Forget it. The tough Irish kid she used to be has come to her rescue.

She sits opposite me, hands clasped between her knees. Again she's examining my face unabashedly. There's no room for reticence here.

"You think they'd give you an aspirin, at least, something. The swelling in your lip seems to have gone down some. Does it hurt?"

"It feels strange, like I've been to the dentist."

"Why don't you try and take a nap? It's a while yet until lunch, I think. God, I can't stand not knowing what time it is. Just plain meanness on their part. What harm would there be in our keeping our watches?"

"So how'd you go from shacking up with a married restaurant-supply salesman to a rich husband and a house in Saddle River?"

"Oh, please, Rita. It was a long time ago."

"Come on, tell me, Mrs. Tyler. Help pass the time."

What happened was Vincent left me. We were up on the boardwalk one night a few weeks after I'd had the abortion. It was hot and the ocean was still, almost worrisome. There was no breeze. We walked along without touching. It was crowded, and everybody seemed out of sorts. I remember the heat and the heavy air, the tinny music and the barkers.

Vincent's car was parked under a streetlight. We stood by it, and he put his hands on my shoulders. He said he was sick about what he'd done to me. "You're a young girl," he said. "Your whole life's ahead of you. The best thing I can do for you now is leave you alone." A big lie, of course. Nobody bails out for the good of the other person. If you want somebody, you'll drag him through anything.

He told me nobody had to know what happened between us. "You'll meet a boy and get married. Don't tell him. Ever. No matter how close you feel to him, no matter how much you believe he loves you and will understand, keep your mouth shut. Listen to what I'm telling you," he said.

He wanted to drive me home, but I wouldn't let him. I couldn't bear to have him nursing me after the fact. I told him to get away from me. I told him to go to hell.

The walk home was long. Boys out for a good time slowed down and shouted at me from their cars. "I've got something for you," one yelled. Something for me. Right. I thought of Vincent's penis the first time I'd seen it and shouted back, "Big deal." The boys in the car thought that was great, of course. "Yeah, it's big, baby, and it's all yours."

I was in my waitress uniform, and my feet hurt. I wanted more than anything to go after Vincent and tell him I didn't care what he did to my life, so long as he didn't disappear from it.

Months, Rita. Months and months went by. I waited for him to call or show up. Every single night at the restaurant I believed he would. Tonight, I'd think as I was combing my hair or tying my apron. I counted on seeing him when I came around corners. In the middle of filling a tray of glasses with ice or folding napkins, I'd stop and say his name to myself, yell it out in my head. After work, ground down, I'd walk by other hotels looking for him. I'd call from pay phones and ask if he was registered, search parking lots for his car. I think he must have had his territory changed, which makes me feel a little better. Maybe it wasn't easy for him. I hope not. I hope it tore him up.

I worked as much as my boss would let me, took every shift I could get. Vincent would look for me at the hotel, I knew, so I wanted to be there all the time. My mother thought I was working so much to help out—I turned my money over to her—but I didn't give a damn about that. It was a convenient excuse, made me look good. I wanted to be where Vincent could find me.

My father was on a skid. The bar he worked at changed hands, and the new owner fired my father for drinking on the job. He stopped taking care of himself, didn't wash or change his clothes. My mother slept with Margie and me every night. She and I kept things together. One night she told me she was putting money aside for me, for when I got married. "A dowry," she said, sounding more Irish than usual. "A little something."

"Don't do that," I snapped. "Spend that damn money, Ma. I'm never getting married."

"Oh, you'll get married," she said, and there was something chilling in her voice. She wasn't encouraging me or trying to give me confidence. She was telling me to take my medicine, live in the world.

"It's my money," I said, "so hand it over. Right now. I want that money, Ma."

I was a breadwinner, so she couldn't mess with me. The next day she left an envelope on my dresser with my name on it. I went out and bought a dinette set, kitchen curtains, and brass canisters, flour, sugar, coffee, tea. My father came home drunk a few days later, tore down the curtains, smashed the table and chairs. By the time I got home he was passed out and my mother was cleaning up the mess. My brother Jimmy was helping, and Margie was crying her eyes out. We worked half the night. There was flour everywhere. While I mopped the floor, I described the whole incident to Vincent in my mind, told him how tough I had it.

The college boy with the puppet was still after Margie. Richard, his name was. He brought John with him to the house one Sunday.

My mother had to work that afternoon, so she made me stay home to chaperone. I was furious because it was the first Sunday I'd had off in weeks, and I'd planned to go to my cousin's house so she could perm my hair. Later I found out the whole thing was a setup. My mother and Margie and Richard had all gotten together to find me a date. John was in on it too. He'd come to meet the sister.

Margie's behavior was particularly offensive that day. She flirted with both boys—squealy girlish stuff that set my teeth on edge. Talk normal, I told her a few times. I sat there with a puss on my face, was downright rude. John was a trooper, did his best to make polite conversation. I got the feeling he wanted me to know he was serious like me, not silly like his friend.

The four of us decided to go see a movie, and my mood improved because all of the sudden I was somebody's date just by virtue of there being two boys and two girls. Sitting in the dark theater sipping cold soda, I felt my craving for Vincent ease. I was glad to be with my sister and her dopey friend. I liked having John beside me.

The next day he called. He was so nervous, he kept stumbling over his words. Finally he said, "I'd like to take you out if I could, if you want to go, if it's all right with your mother." Men are never more likeable than when they're asking women out. I used to hear my own sons on the phone and be so proud. The awkwardness of it, the plain bravery.

Once, when my youngest boy was four, he was playing in the yard while I gardened. The other two were in school, and Susan wasn't born yet. There was a group of kids in the street—not the usual neighborhood kids. Somebody's nieces and nephews must have been visiting. Andrew wanted to play with them, but he was shy. He asked me to walk over with him. I took him as far as the curb, then insisted he approach on his own. Every once in a while you like to give your kid a shove, a shot on the back of the head. He hesitated, looked down at his shoes, took a deep breath, skipped out into the middle of the street and said, "Ta-daaa!" He'd done what everybody has to do sooner or later—take a breath, say here I am. When I heard my boys on the phone with girls, I'd always think of Andrew taking the plunge.

Right from the start I knew John and I were cut from the same cloth. People have pitch, like roofs or music. He was a good son, and I was a dutiful daughter. In the movies we would have been the best friends of the stars.

After a couple of dates he took me home to meet his mother. Their house was in Ventnor, a wealthy suburb of Atlantic City. There was a painting with a light over it in the entranceway and a huge mirror on the living room wall. Lorraine wore a caftan, very sophisticated for those days. She had heavy silver bracelets on both wrists. In their house I felt ashamed of my family's apartment, the ratty sofa where John and I sat, my father coming in and out like a boarder.

Lorraine had made beef Stroganoff, and the table was set with cloth napkins and crystal wine glasses. She smiled at me constantly, kept making references to John and me as a couple. You two sit here and relax, she said. You know John. Make John take you here or there. At first I was grateful—his mother likes me!—but as the night wore on, I felt the sharp edge in her enthusiasm. Why was she working so hard?

Lorraine wanted to be the sort of mother who lets her kid go when the time comes. But it had been her and John for so long.

SPLIT SKIRT

Her instincts told her to hold on tight, but she didn't want to listen.

God, I remember sitting on the couch and watching them clear the table. It was like peeking in a window. They moved so gracefully together, like she was the sun and he was the earth. They never got in each other's way.

I married John when I was nineteen. In my wedding pictures my shoulders are rounded, my chin is down. My expression makes me think of somebody trying to dance, somebody who's not a dancer pulled out onto the floor and making a fool of herself.

Lorraine ran the whole show. I pretended not to have opinions about flowers and table linens; I didn't feel entitled to care about such girlish things. That had always been my sister Margie's turf, and I was afraid to speak up because Lorraine was paying for everything. I regretted not letting my mother put money aside for me. I might have been able to buy my own gown, at least. I came into my marriage with nothing but a suitcase. Money matters. Money always matters.

The night I told my mother I wasn't going to be married in church, she slapped me across the mouth. "You're marrying a rich man," she said, "and I'm glad for that. But I'm still your mother. This is still your house. Don't be so fast to turn your back."

Turn my back, exactly. I saw myself pivoting, breaking away. Two bedrooms for eight people, water stains on the ceilings, my father drunk, my mother's arms chapped to the elbow.

While the wedding plans were under way, I found myself going into Catholic churches in the middle of the day, not my mother's church—her priest would have known me—but any Catholic church I happened by and found open. It would take a minute for my eyes to adjust to the dark, and in those few seconds of blindness I'd feel taken in, acknowledged, seen. As far as anyone knew, I was the young bride-to-be, showing off her engagement ring, about to leave her parents' house for her husband's, nervous, maybe, but happily so. In church my trepidation came to the surface. It was like the moment in a doctor's office when you surrender the arm or knee or breast that's been worrying you and he says, "Let's have a look."

My mother asked me to have a second service in church. She blurted out the question while I was packing my clothes, then waited in the doorway for an answer. I said no, took mean pleasure in it. Why didn't I do it just because she wanted me to? Why wasn't I at least kind?

The wedding was at Lorraine's house. A judge Lorraine was dating at the time performed the ceremony. My family sat off to one side, cowed by the grandness of the place. My father and the boys looked nervous but well scrubbed, their shirts gleaming white and starched. My mother wore a gray dress with a lace collar that she'd had for years. She didn't even buy a new dress, I thought when I saw her. Only Margie made forays into the crowd.

On my wedding night I had to fake virginity. Imagine that. As far as John knew, he was my first boyfriend. I clenched my muscles and winced and gasped, made him stop a couple of times. It wasn't easy. I was an experienced woman, remember. Keeping myself in check took concentration and all my will. What a relief it was to let go, finally, after a couple of nights of holding back. John assumed he'd awakened this feverish passion in me, not a bad thing. A man who believes he's a great lover has something to live up to.

SPLIT SKIRT

We went to Miami Beach for our honeymoon, to a hotel Lorraine and John had gone to for years. I had never been on a plane before, had never been outside New Jersey except the couple of times my mother dragged us to Philadelphia, where she had a cousin. Overnight I became one of the women I used to wait on. I felt my new status down to my toes. Not only was I a wife, I was the bride of John Tyler. I reveled in the deference of waiters and chambermaids. I'd spent time in hotel rooms before, with Vincent, but that had been illicit, seamy. Now I had the world's endorsement. Old ladies smiled at me in the dining room, and doormen saw me coming. "Good morning, Mrs. Tyler."

As a wedding gift Lorraine gave us one of her houses in Ventnor, the one John had grown up in. John's father had inherited what was left of the Tyler money, frittered most of that away during an adventurous youth, married late, then was killed in a car wreck when he was forty-three. Lorraine took over the original family business, Tyler Machinery. She ran it better than the old man ever had, bought real estate and God knows what else. By the time I married John, Tyler Machinery was the least of it. I didn't have any idea how much money there was until well after we were married. How could I understand money like that?

I've always wondered why Lorraine was so willing to accept me as a daughter-in-law. You'd think she'd have wanted somebody with money or at least social standing. She came from a poor family herself and might have been intimidated by the girls John met in college, although it's hard to imagine Lorraine intimidated by anybody. She probably wanted somebody she could push around.

I quit my waitress job before the wedding. I thought I'd go to secretarial school, learn to type and take shorthand. When Lorraine got wind of my plan, she vetoed it. "You're a Tyler now. You're not going to work in some dreary office."

John took over Tyler Machinery. It was a small plant, and many of the employees had been there since John was a kid. He had an office overlooking the factory floor and was content there. Deep down, I think he knew his mother had tucked him away where he couldn't do much harm—the real action was else-where—but if that hurt him, he didn't dwell on it. John liked running the business, doing careful research before investing in new equipment, modifying a manufacturing process, settling a fracas among guys on the line.

I felt as if I'd been swooped up, carried off, dropped down. That house became my whole world. The house and John. Before we married there'd been more affection than passion on my part. Memories of my first lover would intrude when John kissed me. Boy, did that change when we started sleeping together in our own bed in our own house. Before, sex had been completely separate from the rest of my life. I'd gone to hotel rooms, un-dressed and done things, put my clothes back on and gone home. Once we were married, sex was as much a part of my day as pouring our morning coffee. We made love every night and plenty of other times too. I could feel that changing me, growing me up.

I was either with John or I was alone. I didn't see my family or the people I'd worked with at the hotel. It was like going from a bland but balanced diet to eating only chocolate or dry toast. Intense physical and emotional intimacy or solitude. I'd grown up surrounded by people, crowded, and now I had a whole house to myself from eight in the morning until seven at night.

I'd done plenty of housework in my life but had never been in charge. I wanted so much to be good at it. The moment John left in the morning, I went on duty. What to do now? And now? And now? I'd compile a mental list of the chores I'd completed and run through it over and over to reassure myself I was earning my keep. Neither John nor his mother wanted me to work, but I felt uneasy about staying home. My mother had always worked. So had both my grandmothers. I hear so much talk today about working women, this new phenomenon. Poor women have always worked. I was the first woman in my family who didn't.

My new neighborhood was so much cleaner and quieter than what I was used to. The women in the market seemed graceful, deft, doing what came naturally. I was trying to become something new. I found myself examining women until I found some small imperfection—legs that needed shaving, sweat stains, lipstick flaking off chapped lips.

I was homesick. There were times when everything being new got so tiresome. I missed my mother and Margie, the people at the hotel, my old neighborhood. In my new life I had to pay attention all the time. There were no familiar routines, no voices I knew except John's, and let's face it, I didn't know his all that well.

As the months passed, I moped more and the ardor between us cooled. The permanence of marriage and the routine of his days at the plant became apparent to John. When he came in from work he was often tired, crabby. He had this way of not looking at me when I talked. I'd crowd him until he snapped at me, and then I'd sulk. A couple of times a week I'd make up my mind to leave him, go home and get my old job back. I'd feel certain I'd made a terrible mistake.

Lorraine bought me clothes and had them sent to the house. Cotton skirts with canvas belts, sleeveless blouses, cardigan sweaters, clothes like the women in the supermarket wore. At her suggestion I stopped getting my hair permed, let it grow, and bought ribbon to tie it back. I'd do housework all morning, then take a long shower and put on my new clothes. They were beautifully made and felt good against my skin, but often in the afternoon I'd feel shaky, invisible, scared . . . of what, I didn't know. The only faces I felt confident looking into were the faces of children. Some days I'd get dressed three times. Once in my new clothes, out of them and back into my old, out of the old and back into the new before John got home. He liked to see me in his mother's clothes.

Twice or even three times a week we'd have dinner with Lorraine. John acted strangely in the company of his mother. They'd talk about business. The only time I was part of the conversation was when John would ridicule me, gently. He'd tell Lorraine how I'd bounced a check or left the oven on all night, roll his eyes. He said it was harmless teasing, but it wasn't. John was soothing Lorraine's jealousy and his own guilt. It's still you and me, he was saying to her. I remember sitting at her table unable to answer a question they'd put to me. The two of them eyed me coolly, waiting. I couldn't speak because I knew my voice would crack if I tried, and I refused to let Lorraine see she was getting to me. On the way home John would do penance—hold my hand while he drove, kiss me at red lights.

Five months married and I got pregnant. John lit up when I told him, whooped, went right for the phone to call his mother. Lorraine's response was decidedly less enthusiastic. She made me feel there was something gross, low-class Irish, about my fertility. "You don't plan to have as many as your mother did, do you?"

John made excuses for her, said the prospect of becoming a grandmother offended her vanity. Before then I'd been reluctant to tell him what I thought of his mother and his ties to her. No more. I attacked, said Lorraine was too much in our lives, too much in his heart. I stuck my finger in his chest and said, "She's your mother, but I'm your wife. This baby makes that all too clear to her." John didn't fight back. He sat at the table immobilized, looked as if I'd blown a hole in his understanding of himself and the world.

Lorraine's jealousy cast a pall on my pregnancy. I refused to go to her house for dinner more than once a week. John went by himself. I started returning the clothes she bought me, with good reason. I was pregnant and Lorraine was sending A-line skirts and Bermuda shorts. John did his best to satiate both of us. He'd dote on me all day Saturday, then have dinner with her on Sunday. While he was gone I'd lie on our bed and stew, rehearse litanies against him in my head.

I was alone more than ever, and I found myself dwelling on memories of my first pregnancy and the abortion. I relived the worst moments, couldn't chase them out of my head. Vincent's saying he had two daughters and a son, the awful strangeness of walking into my family's apartment that night as if nothing had happened. John didn't know what to make of me. We'd be riding in the car, and I'd start crying, turn my face to the window. "What?" he'd say. "Please tell me what's the matter."

Lorraine said he should ignore me. "Some women are crazy when they're pregnant. Hormone stew." I could have let things be. John was ready to take whatever I dished out. He walked around looking frightened but determined, the way men do in the face of the mystery of women's bodies. I could have sprouted a tail, and he'd have nodded his head.

There was who John thought I was: the fragile mommy-to-be who needed coddling. And there was the real me, furious at him for not standing up to his mother, sick with my own guilt and grief. For the first time since the abortion I allowed myself to calculate how old that baby would have been. Two years and four months. A sentence formed in my head, word by word: I didn't even know you.

The long days alone really turned on me. I'd get up and feel all right, no morning sickness. Today I'll stay on track, I'd tell myself. In the midst of some chore or errand, washing dishes or standing on line in the bank, the sadness would hit, and all I'd want to do was go to bed. So many nights John came home and found the house a mess and me asleep. He'd tiptoe into our bedroom to check on me. I'd hear him making himself something to eat and think if I had to talk to him I'd go crazy.

When he held me I wouldn't let myself be comforted because he didn't know the truth.

One night John woke up and found me sitting in the chair beside our bed. He was bleary, but still he got up and took my two hands. "What?" he said. "What?" By this time he said that without expecting a response, the way you might say it to a crying baby.

"I had an abortion when I was seventeen."

His fingers tightened around my wrists. "What are you talking about?" he said. He was wide awake, his voice low and menacing.

I tried to tell him the story, but before I could get ten words out he yanked me up and shook me by my wrists. I struggled to get free, but he was too strong for me. He smacked my face and shoulders and breasts with my own hands. Honest to God, I thought my wrists would snap. "The baby," I was screaming. "John, the baby."

He must have heard me, what I was saying must have registered finally, because he seemed to come back to himself. He let go of me, put his raincoat on over his pajamas, and walked out, went straight to his mother's house.

For about a week I tried to make it on my own. I got up in the morning, dressed in my old clothes, cleaned, bought groceries, made dinner. There was a park nearby where young mothers

SPLIT SKIRT

took their children. I was obviously pregnant, so I thought I'd fit in there. The women smiled, asked when I was due. Talking to them made me feel worse. Their lives were intact. My husband had hit me and was back home with his mother.

One morning I woke up knowing I was going home. There was nothing like the beginning of a second thought in my mind. I brushed my teeth, pulled on the clothes I'd dropped on the floor the night before, and got on the first bus for Atlantic City. My mother worked second shift, four to midnight, so she'd just gotten up and was standing at the stove waiting for the kettle to boil when I pushed the door open.

"Ma," I said.

She turned around slowly. We hadn't spoken since the day of my wedding. She didn't even know I was pregnant.

"Look at you," she said.

Halfway between the stove and the door I collapsed in her arms. I'd done a lot of crying in the previous couple of months but none of it like the crying I did there in my mother's kitchen. She held me and said okay, okay now, walked me over to the table and eased me down into a chair. She set a place for me, poured tea and a glass of milk, slipped two more eggs into the water. I ate, then lay down in my old bed and slept. When I woke up it was dark outside, and Margie was standing in front of our mirror putting on lipstick.

"Are you moving home?" she asked, though not unkindly. She simply wanted to know what was what.

"No," I said and knew I wasn't. I was going back to my house to wait for my husband to come home. If he didn't, I'd manage. My baby would be born, and I'd take care of him or her with John or without him. There was certainly money enough, and I'd see we got what we needed. A moment in my mother's arms and a good sleep in my old bed had restored me.

Agnes Rossi

A few nights later the sound of a key in the front door woke me. John came into the bedroom, took off his clothes, and got into bed. I'd missed him every second. It was so sweet to have his body beside me again. We lay there feeling the pull, and when I thought I'd die if he didn't touch me, he did. We were both saying sorry, sorry, sorry.

Our love was more intense that night than it had ever been. We were both of us raw. When we finished, John moved away from me, stared up at the ceiling, told me I'd made a fool of him on our wedding night. "You were good," he said. "I believed you." I apologized over and over again while he got up and dressed. When he walked out I wanted to go after him but didn't because I knew it wouldn't do any good.

I spent an enormous amount of money on the baby's room, wrote checks all over town. If John didn't want to live with me, he should at least see evidence of my existence in his bank balance. I had a man come in to paint and wallpaper, ordered white furniture, and filled the closet with baby clothes. When I got into bed at night, my feet would throb from shopping. Sometimes John would arrive, most nights not. Once, as he was dressing to leave, I took his hand and led him into the baby's room. If he saw it, I thought, he wouldn't be able to go. He looked at the crib, the bassinet, the rocking chair. "Who was it?" he said.

I told him the story in a couple of sentences, terrified as I talked that he was going to hit me again. I made sure I was standing in the doorway in case I had to run. When I finished, he pushed past me and went home to his mother.

A couple of days later Lorraine paid me a visit. She walked into the house without knocking and I was reading a *True Story* magazine in bed. Scared the daylights out of me. She told me I'd disgraced her son, entered into the marriage on false pretenses. "The matter would be easily settled if you weren't pregnant," she said and paused. "I will give you ten thousand dollars if you divorce John and sign over custody of his child."

So help me God, I laughed out loud. She looked ridiculous standing in our bedroom, smelling of Chanel No. 5, her enormous black pocketbook on her arm, believing she'd get what she wanted.

"Are you aware that your son has been visiting me at night?" I said.

She wasn't, that much was clear.

"If John divorces me, I'll do whatever I have to do to keep this baby. I'll hire a lawyer, run away, anything."

I called her a foolish old woman; she called me a slut and a liar. After what I'd done, any court in the country would declare me unfit, she said.

I didn't see John for nearly a week. When he did show up, I wouldn't let him touch me. "Your mother was here," I said, and he nodded, sat on the edge of the bed rubbing his face with his hands, offered me no reassurances.

When I went into labor I called John at the plant. He was on his way back from New York, his secretary said, but she'd tell him the moment he got in. I took a cab to the hospital. You'd think that would be awful, right? But it wasn't. All I cared about was getting where I needed to go. In the labor room, I kept asking the nurse if my husband had arrived yet. She'd shake her head and tell me not to be scared, millions of women had done what I was about to do. I was not millions of women. I was convinced the whole bloody process wouldn't work when I tried it. As the hours passed I was sure something had gone horribly wrong. Pain like that couldn't be part of any plan.

When my son was finally born and the nurse put him in my arms, I didn't care a whit where John was or if he ever came back. I slept and woke wanting only my baby. They brought him to me, and I rubbed my lips over his head while he nursed. When John walked in, I cradled the baby closer; and thought, Oh, no, you don't. I think I would have had that reaction even if John had been a devoted husband right along. I hurt all over, I was stitched up, my throat was raw from screaming, and here comes this person who looks like he's just eaten a good dinner. Hah! Get away from my baby, whoever you are.

The three of us went home together. As soon as I walked in, I could tell John had been there the couple of days I was in the hospital. His briefcase was by the door, his sweater on the back of the chair. There were white roses on the kitchen table.

I took the baby into the nursery to change him. John stood beside me, and I showed him how to do it, explaining each step as I went. He stared at the baby and listened, nodding his head. I could tell he was impressed by my skill, which made me glad I'd had so many younger brothers. When I finished, when my baby was clean and dry, John put his arms around the two of us. He said he'd forgiven me and asked me to forgive him. I nodded my head against his shoulder. "It's over now," he said, kissing the part in my hair. "It's over."

"And was it?" Rita says. "Did he ever hit you again?"

"Never. For a long time after, I was afraid he would, but he never ever did. Where I came from, men either beat their wives or they didn't. There was no such thing as one time. Women got married and then found out if they'd gotten a good husband or a bad one. But John was different."

A bunch of women, a dozen or so, walk past our cell, one guard in front, another behind. The inmates are a varied lot— white, black, Hispanic, teenagers, and a couple my age. I look at their faces, wonder if there's a shoplifter among them. Two by two, they're escorted into cells near ours.

Rita smiles at me, crookedly, because of the swelling, the split in her lip. Her smile's as sweet and goofy as a retarded child's. "Some life," she says.

FOURTEEN

*T*he way back to my cell is long, and I'm glad for it. One corridor after another, all with the same tile floor, the same cinder-block walls painted yellow, a guard by my side. Alex has been here and gone. Alex, here. He stood up when I came into the room, said only, Rita. When he reached out with one hand to touch my face, I turned away. Don't, I said.

When the guard came for me, I was lying on my side, book in hand—it felt small and solid, welcoming, its pages porous, and yellow. I was thinking about Emily Brontë, the minister's middle daughter, so wild within, so tame without. I was thinking about moors, about cliffs and ferocious winds and Emily's heart. Some-where I read that she so feared outsiders she once cauterized her own wound with the household iron rather than let Charlotte take her to a doctor. I wasn't so much reading as listening to the sound of Emily's voice in my head when the guard put her key in the door.

"You got a visitor," she said.

My lawyer, I thought. Mrs. Tyler's lawyer had promised to contact mine. I expected chubby Barry in a too-tight suit, starched collar cutting into his fat neck. Barry likes me, thinks I walk on the wild side. I looked forward to his censure, to hearing him say, "What am I going to do with you, Rita?"

I followed the guard up staircases and down hallways. In an open area she was stopped by another guard. They bent their heads over a clipboard, discussed the graveyard shift, midnight to eight. My eyes wandered, then hit on Alex—Alex!—sitting at a small table, waiting.

I squelched the impulse to call out to him. I needed a moment to compose myself. His fist was clenched, and he tapped it against his lips. I could tell that the jail unsettled him, worked his nerves. His forehead was furrowed, his eyebrows up and angled. I know that expression so well. It means a personal state of emergency has been declared; circle the wagons.

What is it about seeing somebody you love when he doesn't see you? It's like feeling sorry for yourself, something like. He looked old. How long had the flesh under his chin sagged? When did the hair at his temples go so gray? His ankles were twisted around the legs of the chair like a high school boy's.

I walked into the visiting room, saw my bruises and fat lip register in Alex's face. Rita, he said as he got to his feet. The pitch of his response didn't sit right with me. My beating was old news. His shock and concern seemed precious, put on, his tone what he might have used with a friend or coworker. I smelled him then, his unique blend of cologne and cotton, shampoo and skin.

SPLIT SKIRT

Alex, I said. I wanted to kiss him. I wanted to fall apart in his arms.

I sat opposite him at a small wooden table. My escort positioned herself in the corner. I expected her to make like a deaf-mute, stare straight ahead, all that. No dice. She looked right at us.

Alex said he'd tried to find out what happened to me, then had called Barry and the warden to get permission to see me. His voice further weakened my resolve. I wanted to touch his arm, at least, put my foot against his under the table. I couldn't. Things between us had gone so far awry that a touch would have been a statement of purpose.

I looked at Alex the way we've always looked at each other when the camouflage has been stripped away finally and we're down to it. I exercised my right to intimacy. He averted his eyes. He monitored himself, as if he'd guessed my appeal might take this form and was ready for me. He'd come with an agenda that required he behave a certain way. This falseness, this manufactured self that he offered, told me what I needed to know.

But because I must have everything spelled out, because I don't trust the information I gather from gesture, expression, and intonation, although God knows I should, I forged ahead, asked him point-blank what was going on.

He was reluctant to answer. I came down here to see if you were all right, he said. That's all. Everything else can wait, Rita, please.

Oh, no. I wasn't going to let him call the shots. If he didn't want to have it out now, I did. If he'd launched into a confession, I'd have said, Not now, Alex. I wasn't going to let him behave well. Whatever he did, I'd have opposed.

He said he was sorry Lee had picked up the phone. He said he didn't know why she did it; he was upstairs, and she beat him to it.

I waited for him to say it had all been innocent. He stared down at his fingertips lined up on the edge of the table.

What are you saying?

I'm in love with her.

Since when?

He exhaled loudly, ran his hands through his hair.

Answer me, Alex.

Months, okay?

He said some more things—something, something. He said he wanted a divorce.

I said motherfucker and cocksucker because I'd heard them yesterday and because I'm a girl in jail and because I knew Alex would wince. The split in my lip opened. Blood ran down my chin, and I wiped it with the back of my hand.

Alex asked the guard to get me a washcloth or something. She left and came back with a wad of paper towel. It felt cool against my mouth. I could taste the wet paper. The guard dabbed at my face, and Alex watched over her shoulder. Get out of here, I said to him. Go.

Always in a story like this one there's the insult to go with the injury. There's the detail you leave out because you're after your listener's sympathy, not her disdain. Alex asked me if I wanted him to pick me up when I got out or would I rather he call my sister Eva and tell her to come for me. I tried to stand up so I could swing at him, but the guard held me down. Just go, she said to Alex, you get out of here.

This guard is walking me, I see now, the way a cop might take the aggressor in a domestic dispute around the block a couple of times, to settle him down. How can anybody work here and be generous? She seems to have been in her job a long time. Her seniority gives her status, but she doesn't swagger. Her hair is short, her skin is fair, her eyes are watery blue. Somebody has to be in charge here, her demeanor says, it might as well be me—better me than some of the others. She wasn't in the dayroom yesterday. I don't believe she would have let the others do what they did to me.

We walk past cells identical to mine. Some of the women recognize me. They look with derision, sympathy, or plain gratitude for the fight yesterday, for something to watch, to talk about afterward. I don't mind being stared at; I like having distinguished myself here. Attention is all. When Rita goes to a funeral, my grandmother used to say, she wants to be the corpse.

"I'm going to have to take you back now," the guard says. "You okay?"

"I'm better. Thank you."

"He's a dog," she says. "I could tell that right off."

I smile, pinch my lip so the cut there isn't stretched.

Two young Latino girls, prostitutes, are standing against the bars in the cell next to ours. One looks about fourteen. She's tiny, can't weigh ninety pounds, and wears a ratty black miniskirt and a guinea T, no bra. Her collarbone is more prominent than her nipples. The other is older, chunky in leopard-skin leggings and a glittery gold top. Both wear heavy black eyeliner.

"Mira," the little one says, pointing at me. She stares, smirks, rolls her eyes, and says something in Spanish.

Her fat friend nods, looks me up and down coolly.

I don't exactly return their stares, but I don't look away either. The guard is having trouble with the lock. Come on, I think. Come on. Open the fucking door.

FIFTEEN

$\mathcal{M}$rs. Tyler suspected my visitor was Alex, and wants to hear what he had to say for himself. Her cot buckles with our combined weight. My heart skips a beat, then races. I take a couple of breaths before I talk, but still my voice sounds strange to me, echoey and out of kilter, as if I'm hearing it played back on tape. The pace is rapid, the pauses too long.

From next door come Spanish and cigarette smoke.

Mrs. Tyler listens, looking grave and grim the way people do in the face of a loved one's defeat.

In her face I see the seriousness of my predicament. Her expression says my husband has gone back to his first wife. My marriage is over.

It occurs to me that Alex has never laid eyes on Mrs. Tyler. How can that be?

Agnes Rossi

. . .

The buzzer sounds and I'm grateful. Let's get out of here already, let's get up and go. It's so good to be walking again, to focus on footsteps, my own and the others'. I'm loosening up, feeling some give between my shoulder blades, rotating my hands at the wrists, when I realize the two hookers are right behind us. This scares me more than it should. My back feels exposed, vulnerable. They chatter away in Spanish, and I feel sure they're talking about me.

Lunch is grilled cheese sandwiches taken out of the pan too soon, pale and greasy. The margarine melted but didn't brown. My split lip makes eating tricky; I'll taste blood if I'm not careful. I tear a sandwich in small pieces so I won't have to bite into it whole. The air smells of wet garbage in filthy plastic pails—sour milk, coffee grinds, spoiled fruit.

There's one of the guards who beat me up. My mouth goes dry, my face burns. It's the white one with pigtails. She's standing under the clock, chewing gum with her mouth open. Her hair is bleached sickly yellow, her skin is coarse, her thick arms are folded across her chest.

"What?" Mrs. Tyler says.

I want to tell her, but I'm afraid if I do she'll turn and look, draw the guard's attention. I shake my head to shush her.

The guard is scanning the crowd. Her mean little pig eyes search every table. I tap my feet, look into my lap. Yesterday her face was ablaze. Her teeth are brown and broken. She hissed through them like a lunatic mother with a belt.

I feel her spot me.

Damn it! Why did Mrs. Tyler have to talk to her lawyer about me? He probably made a stink with the warden. Pigtails might have been disciplined—I'll pay for that. Why didn't Mrs. Tyler mind her own business? I want to go back to my cell.

SPLIT SKIRT

What if she comes after me again? She and the other one could set something up so it looks like I broke a rule. What's to stop them from taking me out of my cell tonight?

Where's the other guard, the good one? I look up and pigtails is staring right at me. She pulls the skin under one eye down with her index finger and leers. I grab hold of the flesh of my thigh and squeeze.

Mrs. Tyler talks through lips barely parted. "Don't even look at her," she says. "Rita, honey, I'll be with you every second. If they try to take you out of my sight, I'll scream bloody murder. I'll demand to see the warden."

The warden. Great. Where was the warden yesterday?

The guard is coming toward me now. What I want to do, what I feel entitled to do, damn it straight to hell, is fall apart, sob, lift my bruised face, say, See what you did?

Mrs. Tyler's foot finds mine under the table.

Pigtails is just a couple of yards away now and keeps coming. I see her feet, her pigeon toes in black workshoes like cops wear, her white socks sagging around thick ankles. Her body odor is foul, like she's sweating inside a filthy uniform.

"You don't look so good, Rita," the guard says, grinning. "How does the other guy look?"

"Please leave me alone," I say.

She's in my face, puckering her lips, wagging her head, mimicking me in a nasal falsetto: *"Please leave me alone."*

She lunges at me and I fly backward, smash my elbow into the wall. But she's playing, grinning. Her arms hang down at her sides. Her laugh is unlike any I've ever heard. It's bloodless, completely bloodless, but alive like brakes screeching or fire burning. Alive.

SIXTEEN

*R*ita won't walk with me. I asked her as gently as I could. She shook her head no but barely, more like a tremor than a voluntary action. Everything that's happened in the last twenty-four hours seems to have hit her all at once. I don't want to leave her alone, so we sit side-by-side on the warm ground, our backs against the fence. Rita pushes her hair behind her ears over and over again. Her hands tremble, her mouth is open. She coughs weakly, deep in her throat.

It's much hotter today, more humid too. There isn't one speck of shade here. The afternoon sun beats down on my scalp, my shoulders, the tops of my feet. I can feel the skin on my face beginning to burn already. Rita's T-shirt is blotchy with sweat; there are spots on her chest, rings under her arms. She looks thirsty. I wish I could take her inside and get her a glass of water.

"At this time tomorrow we'll be out," I say.

Rita hugs her knees to her chest.

Two prostitutes lean against the opposite side of the fence. They're more animated than the rest of us, don't seem as wilted, probably because they're so young. They smoke and look over at us, at Rita especially. One of them makes comments to the other. Yesterday I would have lowered my eyes, looked away. Today I return their gaze.

Rita looks at the prostitutes, then at me, and says, "You know they're hookers, right?"

"Of course I know that."

"They're in the cell right next to ours. I saw them on my way back from seeing Alex. They're tough cookies. Don't antagonize them." She puts one cheek against her knee but doesn't close her eyes. *"Stop staring,"* she scolds.

"I'm not doing anything. They're staring at us."

The prostitutes start walking in our direction. They're in short skirts, high heels, leggings. There's a built-in bump and grind. The small one wears red pointy-toed shoes with four-inch heels, the kind you see in a store and wonder who buys.

They do it for money, I find myself thinking. I watch the little one strut and imagine her under the third or fourth or fifth man in as many hours. All that slamming. Her insides must be as soft as overcooked noodles. What's left of a chicken after you make soup. I wonder about the first time. What was that like? She has big, almond-shaped eyes, long lashes. I imagine those eyes open in the dark, absorbing jolts from below. The one in the leopard-skin tights is flushed from the heat. She walks with her mouth hanging open. I can see her leaning over in the front seat of a parked car while a man eases himself out of his trousers.

They stop just twenty feet from us, seem ready to approach.

SPLIT SKIRT

Without exchanging a word, Rita and I get ready. We sit up straight; I make a note of where the nearest guard is. The little prostitute says something in Spanish; they walk past us. I feel Rita relax, retreat.

Unless it cools down, our cells will be stifling tonight. I haven't had to contend with heat like this in years. My house is air-conditioned, so are my cars, all the places I go. Here it's hot like summers when I was a kid. I remember lying next to Margie in our double bed, pinching her if she touched me with so much as a toe, turning my pillow over and trying to fall asleep before the cool side warmed.

By this time tomorrow I will have pulled into my driveway, parked my car in the garage, and walked up the back steps to my kitchen door. I try to imagine the quiet of my house, the cool.

The first thing I'll do is take the longest shower of my life. Ten years ago we had some work done on the house, and our bath-room was my one indulgence. It's bigger than any of the kids' rooms, has a vestibule with a dressing table, a stationary bicycle, a doctor's scale, and three mirrors, like in a department-store dressing room. The toilet is tucked away in its own little alcove. The bathtub is enormous and sits up on a platform in front of a bay window that looks out over our woods. "Room for two," my sister said when she saw it, much to the embarrassment of my daughter, who was nine and hovered in the doorway. Like many women who were pretty and popular when they were young, Margie has become downright bawdy in middle age. She's used to a certain kind of attention and has to work harder to get it now. I've never been able to enjoy my bathroom the way I thought I would while it was under construction. I'm always a little uneasy there. But today I know that when I get home, I'll slide down in that tub, run the damn Jacuzzi without worrying about mixing electricity and water.

When my daughter was sixteen, she had a friend over—Laura, a tall, pretty girl who had finally been asked out by a football player she'd been stalking for months. Elaborate preparations were under way. My daughter acted as handmaiden while Laura groomed herself for this boy. I winced to see Susan on the sidelines. No boys called our house for her. Laura announced that she intended to use an entire bar of soap in the shower and would not come out until she had. I watched Susan nod gravely, saw myself and my sister thirty years before, didn't know what to want for my daughter.

Rita rubs her back against the chain-link fence and closes her eyes. She inhales deeply, and there's a spasm in her throat, the shudder that comes after crying. When my kids made that sound, I knew they were about to give over to sleep.

What would Susan say if she could see me right now? She'd be horrified, of course, and rightfully so. She'd be frightened for me, humiliated.

I have steadfastly avoided considering how my stealing has hurt my children. I've always believed they were buffered by money. In some ways, I think, I was jealous of them because they were rich kids and therefore had an air of entitlement about them, an assumption that good things would come their way. The quality I've never wanted to acknowledge in my children is their guardedness. All four of them are aloof, slow to trust. Our house was one in which the security might at any moment give way. I was the source of that fragility. I taught my children to beware.

I was like a double agent. Most of the time I was responsible for keeping our family afloat. I was the one who was always there, whose job it was to see that there was food in the refrigerator, clean towels in the bathrooms, oil in the furnace. I went to their soccer games, took them to the orthodontist, made sure their college applications were mailed on time. I waited up when they were out late. I worried myself sick some nights, I did.

But all the while I had my habit, my secret life. Except that it wasn't always very secret. There were the obvious tells, the times I got caught and John got furious, there was shouting, then silences. John junior, my good boy, would eye a new belt or bud vase with trepidation. He would wonder. When David was eleven, he fell out of a tree and broke his arm. I was in a psychiatric hospital in Connecticut when it happened. By the time I got home David's cast was grubby, chipped, covered with signatures. It itches, he told me, it itches bad. I showed him how he could use a knitting needle to scratch the places he couldn't reach with his fingers. No, he said, you're not *supposed* to do that. He no longer trusted me to know what was good for him.

Back in our cell Rita goes right for her bed. I wash my face, wet one corner of the towel and press it against the back of my neck, wipe my arms and armpits, hold my wrists under the tap. My mother believed cold water on a pulse point cools all the blood in a body. Is there any ventilation at all in here?

I comb my hair but don't dare spray it for fear of bothering Rita. She's lying on her back, not reading, not sleeping, and certainly not talking. One hand is over her mouth, the other rubs her stomach.

This heat is making our cell smell like a public toilet. There's condensation on the walls, our sheets are damp to the touch.

. . .

Barbecued beef, the woman behind the stainless steel counter said. It sits on the plate in a gelatinous lump, and Rita won't touch it. She hasn't said a single word in over two hours, still keeps her hand over her mouth most of the time. She's slipped away; she's here but not here. She's looking after herself inside herself. I miss her.

"Try to eat something, Rita. You'll be hungry tonight if you don't. Drink your milk at least."

She ignores me, picks the grapes out of her fruit salad nervously. Her eyes dart all around the room; she's watching for the blond guard.

We make our final visit to the dayroom, and there's the usual rush for the telephones. Rita stops, puts her hands in her pants pockets. Women hurry past on either side. Rita watches the lines form, and her chin starts to quiver. "You could call somebody else," I say, "one of your sisters." She sniffs hard, shakes her head.

We sit on the floor, our backs against the wall. My knee rests against Rita's.

It's been twenty years, at least, since I talked to anybody the way I've talked to Rita. Secrecy has become second nature to me. How else could I have maintained two separate realities as long as I have? But there is something about Rita that draws me out. She's all turbulence and jagged edges, her own worst enemy. She doesn't know the first thing about keeping up appearances.

I've always believed in nursing my sorrows privately. One of the reasons I married John, I think, was that I sensed he'd keep to his side of the fence emotionally. I could be solitary without being alone.

Today is Sunday. John is probably at home. He got up this

morning, fixed his own breakfast, glanced at the front page of the *Times,* read the business and sports sections. Wiping ink from the newsprint off his fingers, he looked around the kitchen and wondered what to do with himself today.

Oftentimes, when John finds himself home alone, he puts on work boots and dungarees, takes a walk around our property. I know this because later, when I get back from wherever I've been, he'll tell me the fence that separates our woods from the neighbor's needs mending, or he'll ask me to have the gardener prune the apple trees. On a warm day like today I'm sure he went outside and made his rounds. I think of John in shirtsleeves, alone in our woods, picking up stray beer cans left behind there by the teenagers who sneak in at night. When I close my eyes, I can see the expression on his face, troubled but intent on keeping busy.

I put my hand on Rita's knee and squeeze. "I'll be right back," I say. "You'll be okay here? I won't be long."

My ears are ringing as I walk over and get on line for a phone. My heart's in my throat. God, I would give anything not to have to call collect. Making this call is hard enough. Being forced to involve an operator, a stranger asking John if he'll accept the charges, seems like the world extracting a second pound of flesh. Before I know it, it's my turn.

The receiver is warm. I push the buttons slowly.

He answers before the second ring.

Even the operator seems surprised.

"John," I say. "It's me."

SEVENTEEN

*R*ita watches me as I make my way back. She smiles. I feel shy, self-conscious. John said he'll leave the office right after lunch tomorrow and be home early. Let's go out to dinner, I said, just the two of us. I made a date with my husband.

I take my place beside Rita. She turns, looks at me quizzically for a moment, then says, "Good for you." She leaves it at that and turns her attention back to the two prostitutes we saw out in the yard earlier. They're sitting in front of the television set. One of them is watching us. Her gaze is more curious than confrontational.

"She's pretty," Rita says. "The little one."

"Hard to tell under all that makeup."

"No, it isn't. She's got beautiful eyes. She looks smart, too, much smarter than the other one."

One prostitute nudges the other. They get up and walk toward us. They stop near us just like they did outside. The little one comes one step closer, peers at Rita's face, runs her finger along her own bottom lip. "What happened to you?" she says.

"I got beat up by two guards yesterday."

"No shit?"

"No shit."

The prostitute makes a whistling sound through her teeth. Her friend asks, "What for?"

"I wouldn't hang up the phone when they told me to."

Both girls blow air out through their teeth. Rita and I exchange a fast look. I want to be cautious, know I should probably nip this in the bud if I can, but there's something inviting, oddly familiar, about the dynamic. One couple meeting another.

"We figured your old man did it to you, and then you stabbed him or set him on fire or something, and that's how you wound up here," the big one says. The little one chastises her with a look, exactly the way a wife would a husband who talked out of turn.

Rita shakes her head. "Did you see the big blond guard in the cafeteria at lunchtime? She was one of them."

"No way," the big one says. "Remind me to stay off the phone." She laughs, eyes her friend eagerly.

"Shut up, Madeline," the little one snaps. "Why you got to be so stupid all the time?"

Crestfallen, Madeline picks at her tights. Clearly, she's messed up, missed the mark again. She pulls up her shirt sullenly, takes a pack of Kools from her waistband, lights one, then looks at me like we're in the same boat, like I am to Rita what she is to her sharp-tongued friend. She offers me a cigarette. I shake my head.

Meanwhile, Rita and the little one are paying attention only to each other. The magnetism between them is palpable, exclusionary. They're like two dogs on the street, two three-year-olds in the aisle of a supermarket. Their eyes are locked in cautious recognition.

"My name is Luz," the little prostitute says, slowly, testing the water. "And she's Madeline."

"I'm Rita, and this is Mrs. Tyler."

"Mrs. who?"

"Tyler."

"Whatever," Luz says. She sits down opposite Rita, Indian-style, making no concessions whatsoever to her miniskirt. "How long you two been here?" she asks.

"Since Friday," I say, cutting in because I haven't said anything yet and I don't want them thinking I'm hostile or intimidated. "We get out tomorrow morning."

Luz turns and looks at me like she hadn't noticed me before, like I'm an interesting development. "What did you do? If you don't mind me asking."

"Shoplifting, drunk driving," I say, pointing at myself, then at Rita.

"Soliciting, soliciting," Madeline says, thumb in her chest, then tilted at Luz.

Luz looks at Madeline with exaggerated disdain, giggles, then says, *"Puta!"*

"Puta sucia," Madeline shoots back, a smile spreading across her moon face.

"Whore," Luz translates, confidentially, leaning toward Rita. "Dirty whore."

Rita nods, pinches her bottom lip, smiles. Luz has won her over with that exchange, I can see. I have a sense, suddenly, of the kind of older sister Rita must be. She loves a brat. "How old are you?" Rita says, cocking her head and squinting at Luz. Her voice is at once affectionate and scolding.

"Me?" Luz says brightly. "Twenty."

"Liar. You're no twenty."

"I'm nineteen," Luz says.

"You're full of shit," Rita says, turning away in mock dismissal.

"No, sir. Not that it's any of your fucking business anyway." Luz turns in the opposite direction, runs her tongue along her teeth.

Rita's legs are stretched out in front of her. She considers the situation for a moment, weighs her options, then taps Luz on the knee with her foot, a fast little sideways bop.

Luz flinches.

Madeline sits up straight.

Oh, lord, I think, here we go.

Luz narrows her eyes at Rita . . . grins, and says, "You're a mess."

"No, you are."

All's clear; I can breathe again. They're sparring like adolescents, trading insults because they like each other.

Luz picks up a match, bounces it off Rita's leg. "How old are you?" she says.

"Twenty-seven."

"You got kids?"

Rita shakes her head no.

"Good thing. Don't have none, a mess like you. What about Tyler? She has kids?"

"Why don't you ask her?"

"You got kids, Tyler?"

"Yes."

"How many? A lot?"

"Four, three sons and a daughter."

"That's okay, that's good. You're a nice lady even if you are locked up. No way this one over here," Luz says, rolling her eyes at Rita.

Rita bursts out laughing. The fog, the funk, the gloom evaporate. She's prettier, more animated than I've ever seen her. She shifts her weight, warming to the task at hand, leans in as if she's about to give Luz some valuable advice. "Let me explain something to you," she begins.

"No, thank you," Luz interrupts. "I'm the one better explain something to you, honey, seeing how my face don't have a mark on it. Look at yourself. Whatever you're doing, it ain't working. Anybody can see that. You know what I call somebody like you? *Loca.* Crazy girl. Crazy lady. You don't know how to look out for yourself, I could see that right off. There ain't nothing you could tell me."

Rita's older-sister archness fades away. "I've had a rough couple of days," she says. "A lot has happened."

"Like what? What happened to you, *loca*?"

"I got beat up, for one thing. My husband left me."

"Your husband left you? You been in jail. How do you know?"

"None of your fucking business."

Luz smirks, holds two fingers out to Madeline for a cigarette, lights it, exhales while scanning the room. Her expression is world-weary, philosophical. "I was married once," she says. "Didn't care for it."

Madeline looks at me and shakes her head. Luz shouldn't have seen it—her eyes were trained on Rita—but she did. This kid would have made a great cop.

"Was too, Madeline," she snaps. "Before you knew me, so shut your fat mouth."

Madeline widens her eyes and lowers her head. I pat her hand.

The buzzer sounds and we line up, Rita and Luz in front,

Madeline and I behind. The top of Luz's head barely reaches Rita's shoulder. Her dark hair is thick and curly, slick with styling gel. Her high heels make a racket on the granite floor in the corridor.

"Hard to walk in those?" Rita says.

"They're better than those ugly sneakers you got on your feet."

Madeline smiles at me. We're like two mothers of mouthy teenagers, glad our difficult girls are happy for the moment.

At the entrance to our cell Luz says, "Try not to have too many tragedies happen to you between now and breakfast, huh, Rita."

"Take it easy, Luz," Rita says.

We're in for the night now, our last one. Rita sits on her cot, arms straight back behind her. She looks like she's come around, like she's feeling much better. She smiles in the direction of Luz and Madeline's cell and shakes her head. The crisis has definitely passed. The night may not be so bad after all. The heat will make us drowsy, and we'll sleep straight through.

From next door comes a little hand, waving, palm away, nails bitten to the quick and painted orange. "You over there, mess? You miss me?"

EIGHTEEN

I should have known something was up, Mrs. Tyler. I should have suspected at least. About six months ago Alex called me Lee. We were halfway around a traffic circle; I was driving. He snapped at me, said, "Go, Lee, now. Go." I was crossing three lanes of traffic, so I couldn't respond right away. Once we were back on the regular road, I said, "*What* did you call me?" Alex was mortified. In the close quarters of the car, there it was. He'd called me Lee. "I'm sorry, baby," he said, staring straight out the front windshield as if he expected a rock to come through it.

I told myself it was nothing, a slip of the tongue, but it was probably my first clue. Their affair started then, I'll bet, if not earlier. It must have taken a while to progress to that point. Even the most absentminded person does not begin an affair one night and call his wife by his lover's name the next. Maybe two wives hurries things along.

Alex and I have had our ups and downs. What married couple hasn't? About two years ago we went through a very bad time. It all started when I got fired. I was called into my boss's office and told my department was being cut by 20 percent. He was going to have to let me go. I started crying right there, staring at my boss's plants—he had dozens in his windows, all thriving. You see, I'd known layoffs were coming, and I'd been worried, a little, about the people I thought were vulnerable; I was sure I wasn't one of them. My boss seemed at once irritated and unnerved by my tears. Men seldom understand that crying in a moment like this is not a play for sympathy. It simply means the juices are flowing.

Alex and I had been married a little over a year and had just started looking for a house. I was making decent money, and everything hinged on our joint income. On Alex's salary alone, given child support and debt, we couldn't afford a mortgage payment. I owed thousands of dollars in student loans and thousands more to Visa. Alex was in even worse shape. He and Lee had bought their house at the worst possible moment in history, and they took a bath when it was sold.

We were still living in my little apartment then, but I had the fever: I used to look at small, well-kept houses—the ones with rounded front doors really got to me—and imagine I'd find peace and stability amidst braided rugs, shining hardwood floors, mismatched antique plates standing on their edges.

We'd buy a house, and then I'd have a baby. That was the second part of the dream: me in this humming house with my baby and my husband. The thing was, though, the woman I envisioned wasn't me exactly. She was and she wasn't. In my fantasy future, I'd be different, better. My brow would be smooth, my voice rich and mellow. I'd tap into some as-yet-undiscovered well of emotional generosity and steadiness.

Alex already had two kids, of course, and he was in no hurry to have another. He was willing, but apathetic; he made it clear he'd go along for my sake. Alex knew firsthand what it was to have a child, had already burned through whatever romantic notions he might have had. That's the problem with marrying somebody who's been married before. A divorced person is short on illusions. Alex's reluctance to have a baby hurt. It made me feel like Lee was his true wife and I was just a glorified girlfriend.

Alex said my losing my job was a setback, sure, but we'd get through it. So we'd wait on a house. He was still recovering from his first foray into home ownership and treated real estate agents with a flaky combination of deference and bad manners. Alex liked my Jersey City apartment with its high ceilings and chipped plaster. He felt unencumbered there, a little Bohemian.

One month after I lost my job, Lee announced she'd been offered a scholarship to law school at Stanford, to a special accelerated program for women over thirty-five. She couldn't take the children because she'd be living in a dorm. She wanted Kevin and Marisol to live with us for two years. Alex said yes without talking to me.

I was absolutely stunned when he presented the whole thing as finished business. A few weeks before had been New Year's Eve. Alex and I had had another couple, friends of his from work, over for dinner. I had done everything—the cooking, the cleaning, the shopping. After we'd eaten, after I'd served everybody and removed their plates, Alex asked who wanted coffee or tea. Two teas and two coffees. I fully expected him to take care of it, since I'd done everything else. I was a little self-conscious in front of the other woman, was afraid she'd think I was oppressed, a drudge. I wanted her to see some evidence that Alex and I shared household chores. "Rita," Alex said from the kitchen. "You want to come in here and get the coffee going?" I was embarrassed and angry, but I got up and did it because I didn't want to make a stink in front of our guests.

A couple of minutes before midnight I suggested we turn on the TV to watch the ball come down in Times Square. "No," Alex said. "We're not watching that." The other man said, "Good. I never watch that thing. I don't need to see something on TV to experience it." What I wanted to do had no bearing. The menfolk had made up their minds. I sat there steaming, pressing my thumbnail into the tablecloth and thinking what a raw deal marriage is for a woman. On the one hand your work load gets increased dramatically. I'd spent two days getting ready for that dinner party. On the other, your voice, your vote, your authority is decreased. Before we were married, Alex would never have responded to a suggestion of mine with a dictatorial no. A wife does the work of two adults and has the clout of a child. I should have gotten up and turned on the damn TV, of course, but I didn't.

When Alex said Kevin and Marisol were coming to live with us, I immediately thought of New Year's Eve. When it came right down to it, I realized, Alex assumed he was in charge. But then I felt guilty. I thought, these are his children, his son and his daughter. It was my duty as an adult and his wife to be generous. Actually, I didn't mind their coming so much as I was envious of Lee. I pictured a gang of middle-aged women hunched over fat law books, passing around bags of chips and swigging diet soda. I'd thought about going to law school, had even taken the L.S.A.T.

I was still unemployed, and Alex was getting testy. His eyes were steely when he came in at night. "What did you do today?" he'd always get around to asking. I'd list the chores and errands I'd completed, the phone calls I'd made, the résumés I'd sent. I'd lie like a rug. On this front I welcomed Kevin and Marisol. If I was taking care of Alex's children, surely I'd be entitled to stay home for a while.

We knew we were going to have to move to a much larger place and planned to rent a house—until we priced them. Three-bedroom apartments, even, were out of our reach. I wanted to know why Lee couldn't be made to pay child support, the way we had. "Should we take her to court and lose?" Alex snapped. "You have money for that?" It was a dire situation, something I'd never known before, a true financial crisis. Alex took it hard. I could see the indictment it carried working on him. Was he unable to provide for his family? For my part, I resented being saddled with hardships from Alex's first marriage. These children needing bedrooms, this woman deciding to go to law school and disrupting my life. Also, deep down, I believed as a married woman I was entitled to be dependent on my husband. There, I've said it. For a long time that made me cringe. I thought it was some putrid vestige of feminine weakness. Now I'm not so sure. I may have been fighting the good fight without knowing it. One person, one job, thank you very much.

I was already doing all the work at home. When Alex and I first got together, I was so glad to have a man in my life that I welcomed domesticity, leapt to it. I wanted to take good care of him, and I did. As time went on, though, Alex became more demanding. He expected things done a certain way—fresh spinach, not frozen, never mind that I'd have to spend a half hour at the sink rinsing the damn stuff, sheets changed every Saturday, things like that. Now he was proposing adding two children. I have four younger sisters. I know how much work kids are. Lee had never had a job. She had stayed home and been a mom. With me, Alex thought he had the newer model, the wife who does all the work at home and brings in money too.

I heard a radio psychologist say working mothers talk about sleep the way starving people talk about food. We all smirk about this stuff. It's embarrassing because it's so damn mundane. Except that this is how people live. The way you spend your days adds up to your life. We're not talking here about malaise, women contending with a vague sense of dissatisfaction while dusting. We're talking about physical exhaustion. American women are lurching through their days sleep-deprived.

Men's experience, equally boring, is considered reverently, deemed a worthy subject for art. *Death of a Salesman,* for Christ's sake. The toll corporate America takes on the souls of its workers. If old Willy Loman had to haul groceries home, turn on the oven before he took off his coat, make a fucking meat loaf, he'd have died much sooner.

I should be grateful to Lee. She wants her family back now? She can have them. Let her be a lawyer *and* the one everybody stares at when there's no toilet paper in the house. I'll keep my wretched job, but when I get home I'll eat a slice of pizza and take a hot bath. Saturday afternoons I'll spend in the library instead of the grocery store.

As the day Lee was due to leave for California drew near, Alex got more and more depressed. His libido about disappeared. That felt manipulative too. He was withholding sex because I wasn't earning money, like a wife might. God, things were complicated. He'd turn his back in bed, and I'd feel like I was just making one more demand: Fuck me.

You know why I didn't get off my duff and get a job? Revenge.

SPLIT SKIRT

Alex hadn't included me in any of the negotiations. He'd blithely gone ahead and agreed to the kids' coming. Why should I knock myself out making his agenda work?

Alex's mother saved our necks by offering us her house in Greenwood Lake. Moving there would mean a long commute for Alex, but we could live for almost nothing, just utilities. I would take the summer off. Off! I'd been brainwashed. Care for two kids, and you're said to be taking time off. Anyway, I was so glad to have a house—granted, it was my mother-in-law's and she would have liked to sell it out from under us if she could only find a buyer—but I didn't concern myself with particulars. I finally had this thing I'd been lusting after since I was twelve. We kept our apartment so Alex wouldn't have to drive the eighty miles every night.

The first day there Alex built a fire to dry the place out. Then he went fishing. I scrubbed floors, washed walls and windows, took bedding and curtains to the laundromat, then hung them in the sun to dry. There was one of those clothes-drying contraptions in the backyard, the kind that opens like a beach umbrella. I vacuumed the insides of closets and cabinets, took down pictures and put up my favorites from home.

Kevin and Marisol stuck together at first. I remember them lying on their stomachs playing Chutes and Ladders, a game much beneath Kevin. They'd hover around Alex, but me they steered clear of completely. Everything will be fine, I told myself, they'll adjust. I liked the idea of spending time alone with these two strange kids who'd just been sent packing by their mother.

A couple of weeks went by; the kids and I were still uneasy in each other's company. When I walked into a room, they'd turn and look at me as if to say, "Yes, Rita, what is it?" There's nothing like a child's indifference to make you feel invisible.

After the first few weeks Alex got very busy at work and

almost never came up to the lake on weeknights . . . wait a minute
. . . no, Lee was in California then, at least I think she was. I never
pressed Alex about why he had to stay in Jersey City so often. It
was a kind of egomania on my part. For all I know, he stashed
me away up there on purpose.

I was lonely, so I'd venture out in the daytime. It's a scary
place, Greenwood Lake. Most of the houses are rundown, the
people clannish. A lot of N.R.A. bumper stickers on pickup
trucks and filthy upholstered furniture on porches. People would
stare at me as I walked by, give me stingy little nods. I felt as if
I were in some 1970s movie about a bunch of townspeople who
have a disgusting secret, they eat each other or something, and
I was the outsider snooping around.

Our house was right on the lake, and Marisol couldn't swim.
She was just five, and terrified of the water. She refused to get her
head wet. The first couple of weeks, I'd panic when she was out
of my sight, especially when Alex wasn't there. I'd be sure she'd
found her way to the water's edge and lost her footing.

Every morning I'd help her into her bathing suit, and she'd
spend the day by the kiddie pool, a small cement circle in the
sand by the lake. Kevin was a good swimmer. He'd learned while
his family was intact, back when his parents had time to concern
themselves with extras like swimming lessons. He would aban-
don Marisol for a group of local boys who roughhoused in the
deep end. They'd swim out to the raft and sit straight-armed, feet
dangling in the water.

Marisol used to fill her pail with water from the kiddie pool,
carry it twenty or thirty feet, dump it in the dingy sand. Over and
over again. She went at it with steady determination, like it was
her job. There was an old guy, an employee of the town, who saw
what she was up to. He'd keep an eye on the water level, and

when it got low, he'd turn on the hose and fill the pool with clean water. Marisol would stop long enough for him to do it and then she'd start back in. They had an understanding, the old man and the little girl. You fill and I'll empty.

One morning as we were getting ready to go I was rubbing sunscreen on Marisol's shoulders. Her skin was delicate, and I made sure I kept her well greased at all times. "You know, Marisol," I said, "I can teach you to swim."

She looked embarrassed and relieved, as if not being able to swim was a secret she'd grown tired of keeping. I sat down beside her on the bed. She got up and stood in front of me so we were eye-to-eye.

"You know how to teach me?"

"Sure. I've taught lots of kids. My sister when she was smaller than you."

"Yeah?" she said skeptically.

Marisol cried at night for her mother. I'd go to her when Alex wasn't there, but she'd turn to the wall and scream until I got out of her room. Lee called every couple of days, but Marisol would say only a few words to her, in a voice that was barely audible. Lee would have to ask her to repeat herself, speak up. I knew I should tell Lee about the crying, since Alex refused to, but I didn't. Marisol had her reasons for keeping her pain from her mother, I told myself. But the truth was that I wanted to be the one to comfort her.

I had never actually taught anybody to swim, but I had a clear idea of the method I'd use—desensitization. I would not rush her. She'd set the pace. I'd have the patience of a scientist. The first week we did nothing but walk around the shallow end.

Sometimes Marisol held my hands, sometimes I carried her. She'd wrap her legs around my waist and squeeze. When we got out, she'd be so stiff she'd stagger her first few steps.

I thought we'd sit together on the sand, but we didn't. As soon as we got out of the water, Marisol would wander away. *Wander* is too soft a word. Marisol would walk straight away. She'd stopped bailing out the kiddie pool and was now filling her pail with sand in one place and dumping it in another. Back and forth she'd go. It was hypnotic, watching this little girl work.

Kevin, Marisol, and I ate dinner in front of the TV. At first I insisted we sit at the table but gave up on that when it was clear nothing was even starting to happen. We'd eat whatever I selected from the deli counter at the very grand local supermarket: barbecued chicken, stuffed peppers, seafood salad. Everything looked great, but none of it had much taste. I couldn't help thinking the officers of the Shop-Way corporation had made a mistake putting such a fancy store in so depressed an area. There was a whole aisle devoted to cheese, a coffee bar, a produce section so vast it gave one the feeling of shopping in an open-air market.

Kevin and Marisol would watch old situation comedies blankly, rarely smiling, never laughing. By ten o'clock they'd both be in bed. I'd hang in with the TV or read awhile. I had trouble staying with a book, and usually would end up leafing through the stack of women's magazines Alex's mother had left behind—*Women's Day, Ladies' Home Journal, Family Circle,* all from the sixties. The pages were mildewed and porous and had lost their sheen. The stories and advertisements were dated, campy. Women had elaborate hairdos or knee socks or both. One editorial implored women to call the rooms where they relaxed with their husbands and children "family rooms," not "dens." "Den" sounded so heartless, the writer claimed, compared to the warm and welcoming "family room."

I'd make myself a vodka and tonic or juice and sit out on the front porch. I had some pot I'd bought on the sly just before moving up. I'd smoke part of a joint and consider the arbitrary nature of existence. There I was, sitting on somebody else's steps minding somebody else's children. I'd shiver and stretch, think about calling one of my sisters. I'd know that I should call Alex, but most nights, if Alex didn't call me, we didn't talk.

The months before we moved to the lake had been stormy; Alex and I had had a series of nasty fights. Our fuses were short; one snide remark from either of us, and a whole day would be ruined. Alex was always saying he wanted peace, wanted us to get along. What he meant was that I should agree with him always. The minute I balked about anything, there'd be trouble. Alex would have wanted me to call him from the lake and tell him everything's fine, the kids are great, we had a terrific day. He didn't want to hear that I was bored and lonely, stuck up there in that weird community with nobody to talk to but a couple of kids who didn't have much to say to me.

The physical distance between Alex and me was significant. I was beyond his sphere of influence, outside his range. After a week or two I got used to sleeping alone. For the first time in years I began thinking of myself separate from him.

I used to sit out on that porch until midnight or one o'clock. There were wind chimes, I remember, fucking wind chimes tinkling off in the distance. Spineless and sentimental, the sound of self-pity. If I had a second drink, I'd consider hunting them down and vandalizing them.

· · ·

It was the middle of July before Marisol let me stand in her doorway while she cried. Some nights the sound broke my heart—utter desolation in a dark house. Other times I'd be too tired to feel much, and I'd simply wait for her to stop so I could go back to bed. I crept into her room gradually—leaned against the dresser one night, stood by the bed another, and finally sat down and massaged her back so she'd settle down and we could both get some sleep.

On Friday mornings I'd clean the house. In the afternoon I'd plan, shop for, and cook a real dinner. By six o'clock the kids and I would be listening for Alex's car. When he finally came through the door at seven or seven-thirty, Marisol would shout, "Daddy's home!" and run for him. Alex would scoop her up, kiss her over and over, look handsome and worldly in his suit minus tie. We'd eat dinner at the table, go out for ice cream after, and then Kevin and Marisol would go to bed.

Friday nights always had such promise. Four days apart made us reach for each other with genuine longing. We'd start out ardently, passionately. But it was like we couldn't get close enough. Some hard-edged combination of disappointment and anger crept in, made us brusque, scrappy, violent. Under the guise of hot sex, we manhandled each other, pushed, scratched, bit. He came, I came, it didn't matter. We were both deeply dissatisfied.

After Alex was asleep, I'd lie there and wish it were a week-night and I was alone, free of Alex's grasp and his voice and his license to command my attention. Living apart from him during the week, I got used to spending time alone. I'd get the strangest feeling lying awake in the dark while Alex slept. I'd begin to feel that my outline was blurring, that I was getting murky like the water in the lake. I'd lie there and listen to the goddamn wind chimes and wish I were out on the porch smoking a joint. I'd try to slip out of bed, but Alex is a light sleeper. He'd fidget, slide one leg over my two.

Come Sunday Alex would be eager to leave. He'd make a big production of getting ready, tap stacks of work papers on tables, ask me where his keys, wallet, and sunglasses were. Why are men always asking women where things are? Who put us in charge of minutia? Once I fell asleep after dinner, and Alex came into the room and woke me up to ask where his toenail clippers were. I stared at him, marveling, really, at his nerve. "Never mind," he said sheepishly. "I'll find them myself."

The only time I felt good that summer, the only time I felt calm and focused, was when I was giving Marisol a swimming lesson. I'd hold my hands under her stomach when I taught her to kick, watch her serious expression while she practiced blowing air out through her nose. If I slept past eight, I'd wake up to find her staring at me. "Get up, Rita," she'd say. "We have to go soon."

One night Alex came up to the lake when he'd said he was going to stay in Jersey City. He walked in to find us all dozing in front of the TV. Marisol was too groggy to give him her usual greeting. He sat down, switched the channel to a ball game, then started complaining bitterly about the snow on the screen and the picture flipping. He went through the full no-aerial ritual, wire hanger, swearing, tin foil sculpture, everything. The kids and I just worked around the bad reception, watched whatever came in reasonably well. That night we'd been having a particularly harmonious evening in our sluggish way, until Alex burst in and made trouble. "You know, Alex," I said, "we were fine here until you showed up." He was slapping the side of the television and sputtering like a madman.

"Get cable," he said. "Tomorrow. Call 'em up."

So I did. I called 1-800-OK-CABLE, and a blond twenty-two-year-old was dispatched to my door. I've got news for you, Alex. News.

He had a coil of cable on his forearm and a tool belt around his waist. One of those nice suede ones—well worn, nubby. I smiled and wished I'd taken a shower that morning; I was glad I'd opened the door wearing just a long T-shirt and undies. I smiled and smiled and smiled, and so did he.

We went smilingly into the den. He crouched down like a catcher at the plate, and I crouched beside him. He asked me where I was from. "Not here," he said, meaning I was obviously from someplace better. "Oh no, not here," I said, meaning you're right, I'm much too sophisticated to be from this place.

I was acutely aware, suddenly, of Kevin and Marisol in the kitchen eating Cheerios and of how important it was that they stay put. Right on cue, as if they knew their father's territory needed protecting, they tromped in with their bowls and stood looking at me and the cable man. "Cute kids," he said. "My husband's from a previous marriage," I said. They spooned cereal into their mouths and chewed.

He went about the work of installation. I watched him unabashedly, more than unabashedly—strategically. I stood on the porch while he climbed a pole in the street. He advanced from one peg to the next so easily. Marisol pestered me to get a move on so we could go out to the lake. I blew her off. "I'm nowhere near ready," I snapped. "So relax. Go play in your room or something."

It's a fine thing, Mrs. Tyler, a young man at the top of a telephone pole, leaning back from the waist, blue sky and green leaves behind him. He looked down at me, took off his shirt, wiped his face with it, and stuck it in the back of his jeans.

Kevin left to find his buddies. Marisol was sulking in her

room. My cable man climbed down and asked for something to drink. Iced tea? Iced tea would taste so good right now. I took the two best glasses from the cabinet and a tray of ice from the freezer. It was the old-style ice-cube tray—metal, with a handle that just wouldn't budge. He took the tray out of my hands and so easily freed those cubes. One, two, three, four in each glass, brown tea over, and a lemon, cut, cut again, squeezed. He was bare-chested and just a little gamey with morning sweat, Ivory soap still in the mix. I made the first move, put my hand that was cold from holding my glass on the muscle between his armpit and nipple, pressed in hard with my fingertips. "Yeah?" he said, and there was wonder in his voice.

We fucked in the kitchen without a condom and with Marisol down the hall. He pushed my T-shirt up, my panties down, lifted me onto the counter. Off came his tool belt, down came his fly. It was a quickie to be sure, but a good one. After he came, we leaned against each other for a moment, his forehead on my shoulder. "My name's Brian," he said.

"Rita."

"I know. I heard the little boy say it."

Our voices broke the spell. There I was in the kitchen with a stranger, a workman. No condom, I was thinking, no condom. I wanted him out of my house so bad. "You have to go now," I said. "I'm sorry, but you really do have to go." I signed a work order; he gave me my copy and left.

In the bathroom I washed my face and hands, looked at myself in the mirror. "You are a mental case," I said to my reflection. "You need to be put in an institution for life or killed." I skulked into Marisol's room. She was lying on her floor coloring. "We can go now?" she said brightly.

What a day. I couldn't believe what I'd done. I was frantic about forty things at once. Getting caught. The cable man would

145

tell somebody, and the somebody would tell Alex. AIDS. Suppose Brian ran around shtupping all his lonely and pathetic customers. What if he were bisexual or used drugs intravenously?

My God, has Alex been sleeping with Lee *and* me? Who else has she slept with? We may all be dead soon. At least I worried about it, not enough to be honest, of course, but plenty. Has my safety ever crossed Alex's stinking mind? Maybe he's been mean to me since my arrest because he thinks I had sex with Paul and Lee won't sleep with him if he sleeps with me. Life is disgusting.

I'd left a perfectly good diaphragm in my night-table drawer and let this strapping young man come inside me. Twenty-two, Alex, tall and blond and handsome. I imagined bringing up the cable man's child as Alex's, prominently displaying every old photograph of blond-haired relations I could squeeze out of my mother, maybe inventing some. I could go to antique stores and buy pictures of fair-skinned people, tell Alex they were my great aunts and uncles.

And then there was Marisol. Had she left her room at any point? She seemed pretty settled in there with her coloring book and crayons, but how could I be sure? Maybe she'd walked in on us and was already in the process of repressing the memory. I'd have to watch her carefully for signs of trauma, see if she got agitated in the kitchen. What if she'd seen but hadn't repressed? What if, at the dinner table Friday night, Marisol said, "Daddy, the cable man pulled down his pants and put Rita on the counter."

We got into our bathing suits and went out for our lesson. I was in a daze and just went through the motions. Marisol floated on her back, eyes closed, mouth open. I looked down at the V in her bathing suit, at her little-girl pussy, and thought about when mine was like that, a sweet hairless slit.

That night I made dinner for the kids—real food, no takeout

for us. I'm not a good cook, so it wasn't much of a gift. I made great big burgers and tried to make french fries from scratch. What a disaster. As each layer of potato cooked, it detached itself from the whole and bonded to the surface of the pan. We walked to Dairy Queen after dinner. I wanted Kevin and Marisol close to me. I would have held their hands if I thought they'd let me.

Every so often an image of Brian would intrude on my guilt. The light in his eyes when I first touched his chest, his tan hands on the edge of the countertop, the way he'd taken note of my name.

I kept the kids up way past their usual bedtimes because I was afraid to be alone with my thoughts. By eleven o'clock they'd had enough of my manic good cheer; they huddled on the couch and fell asleep. I poured myself a vodka on the rocks and took my position out on the porch.

The lake was still, the air warm and moist. I took a swallow of vodka that made my eyes water. I'd had sex with another man. His penis had entered my vagina. I couldn't even say I'd been swept away by lust. During the couple of seconds it took Brian to position himself between my legs, I'd been absolutely clear-headed. Into that moment of acute self-awareness had come the first thrust. A seal had been broken, a sacred pact violated. What had Alex been doing while I was getting fucked on his mother's counter? Sitting at his desk? Waiting for the elevator? Buying a newspaper?

I decided I'd call the cable company in the morning to find out how to get in touch with Brian, then ask him to have a test for H.I.V. I'd tell Alex I was tired of the diaphragm and insist we switch to condoms with Nonoxynol-9. I didn't know what I'd do about oral sex or the days during my cycle when we normally didn't use anything.

I heard a car door shut, footsteps. Alex, I thought. I stood up, straightened my clothes, rubbed my eyes, and waited. The second I saw Brian, I knew I'd been hoping he'd come back.

"Blah, blah, blah," says Luz from next door. "Who cares who you were humping, Rita? Did the little girl learn how to swim?"

Mrs. Tyler and I look at each other. She smiles and shrugs. Her face is flushed in the fluorescent light.

"She did," I say. "While all that was going on, Marisol learned how to swim."

It was a Sunday afternoon. Alex made a remark about how little vodka was left in the bottle and asked if I had a boyfriend who drank. I was feeling mean—he was bustling around, getting ready to go—and guilty too. Brian and I *had* drunk most of the vodka. In front of the kids, I told Alex to go fuck himself. We had a terrible fight. I said I was sick to death of being stuck up in the woods while he lived like a single man in Jersey City. He said he was tired of my moodiness, my constant complaining. He was the one who had it hard, driving back and forth, being alone all week. I stormed out, went and sat on the dock.

Now here comes Marisol, the flip-flops we bought in the supermarket slapping against the soles of her feet. She's got her pail and shovel and is about to start moving sand. "Come over here," I tell her.

She sits down beside me with her legs straight out in front of her, stares at the daisies on her sandals for a moment, then looks out at the water. "You're teaching me to swim," she says, her voice airy and matter-of-fact. "I'm learning how to swim."

SPLIT SKIRT

The day I got arrested I was walking on a street near where I work, and I saw a little Chinese girl who refused to go into a store even though her father was screaming at her. You remember, Mrs. Tyler. This kid was really something. She wouldn't budge. That day on the dock Marisol had the same kind of autonomy and grit. She was showing me how a self-respecting girl behaves.

We waded into the water for a lesson, and it happened. I let go of her, and she paddled furiously, nose to the sky like a hound. Expending enough energy to float ten Marisols, she managed to keep her head above water.

Alex came outside, dropped his suitcase, and cheered. He didn't go back to Jersey City that night. We had a cookout in Marisol's honor. Alex held her on his lap while Kevin and I presented her with an Olympic-style ribbon, a Hershey's Kiss stapled to a shoelace. Overwhelmed by all the fuss, Marisol scrambled down from Alex's lap, pulled the chocolate free, and popped it into her mouth.

Alex and I sat outside and talked until after midnight, shyly at first; we were out of practice. He said he was scared, asked me if I knew our marriage was in serious trouble. He started to cry. He said that when he thought about me sleeping alone in our bed, his heart ached, he loved me so much, but then, come Friday night, he'd be nervous driving up to the lake, worried about the sort of reception he'd get from me. "You never seem glad to see me," he said.

I told him living up there depressed me, made me feel disoriented and cut off from him. I was homesick and needed to go back to work. I said I was sorry I hadn't been more help when we didn't know where we were going to live.

We decided to move back down as soon as we could. I'd find a job, we'd borrow money if we had to. We held hands on the way to bed, and that night we didn't grab at each other. We used the pads of our fingers, the palms of our hands. The next morning I walked him out to his car, and we made out for ten minutes on the driveway. The last thing Alex said to me before he pulled out was, "Call me tonight, Rita, no matter what." And I did. I called him.

NINETEEN

*J*ohn junior was born in 1960. The first couple of months of his life are a blur. He was all I cared about, this lump in the crib, this tiny boy. He was a terrible baby, as babies go. I don't think he slept more than an hour at a time until he was six months old.

When my brothers were babies, they seemed indestructible. Feed them when they howled, change them when they stunk, but this baby, my child, was fragile. His remaining alive from one minute to the next depended on my constant vigilance. He was all curled in on himself; blue veins showed through his thin skin. There was that belly button thing, and the scab on the end of his penis. Circumcision. Men have the tips of their penises cut off without anesthesia just hours after they're born. Welcome to the world, snip, snip. Physical trauma like that has to leave psychological scars. I don't think they ever fully recover.

When John junior finally settled down some, when night and day were distinct again, I got mopey. It was as if I'd returned from an arduous journey only to find ordinary life dreary. The first thing that goes when you have a baby is your ability to walk out the door. A couple of times when John junior was asleep I'd decide to run an errand and have my coat on before I remembered he existed. I told my husband I was getting cabin fever, so he brought home a beautiful baby carriage, German, engineered like a Mercedes. This thing hugged corners, absorbed jolts. I'd put the baby in it after his morning nap, and off we'd go.

I gained over forty pounds while I was pregnant. After the baby was born, the only clothes I could get into were my maternity dresses. My husband told me not to worry—he was a breast man. He'd gaze at mine when I got undressed, reach for them in the kitchen, the car, the moment I had both feet in bed. Ashamed of being fat and preoccupied with the baby, I didn't want John touching me at all. His feelings got hurt, and he became more aggressive. Why don't men understand that if a woman is skittish, they have to go slow? When John pawed me, what had been a blank in me, an absence of desire, turned to anger and disgust. Men do what they want done, I suppose. A man who found himself indifferent would love a woman to pull a sack over his head and ravage him.

I needed new clothes. As much as I'd resented my mother-in-law's gifts, I was uneasy about shopping for myself, afraid my tastes weren't refined. I decided I'd go only to a snooty little store in Ventnor, Edith Clark's. Anything I bought there would pass muster.

It wasn't a very pleasant place, small and dark, and I took an instant dislike to Edith. She wore too much face powder and flowery perfume, had droopy breasts and bony calves, clutched a lace hankie in one hand. Her bowing and scraping set my teeth on edge. She was sixty, I was twenty, and she called me Mrs. Tyler. I kept going back because I was afraid to go anyplace else. Left to my own devices in a larger store, I might think something was pretty, buy it, bring it home, and have John or his mother say it was tacky or garish. I went to Edith Clark's for an education.

One afternoon I was in the store with the baby. I'd been eating grapefruit and drinking black coffee, hoping to go from a size fourteen to a twelve, but I couldn't button the forest-green pleated skirt Edith had set aside for me. This shouldn't have been a big surprise. I'd been sneaking Heath Bars and Tastycakes while I was out with the baby, but I'd hoped these wouldn't register somehow. I leaned in toward the mirror, puffed out my cheeks, turned around and looked over my shoulder. Jesus, Mary, and Joseph, was my rear end big! I called myself a fat cow and got dressed.

Edith was peering into the carriage cooing at John junior as I came out of the changing room. She genuinely liked him, would often follow me around the store with him in her arms. He was gurgling up at her, reaching for her pearls, when the door opened and in walked a woman with teased hair, false eyelashes, and frosted lips. She said she was looking for a car coat, white or pink, with big round buttons. Edith waited until the woman's voice trailed off, then said, "A car coat?"

The woman nodded. "A short coat, you know, a long jacket?"

"Just a minute please," Edith said and turned to me. "Is the skirt all right, Mrs. Tyler? I have a lovely cream-colored blouse to go with it."

I told her I didn't care for the skirt; I didn't tell her it was too small, mind you.

Edith looked perturbed, then turned back to the other woman. "My coats are on that rack there. Have a look."

The woman smiled, walked over to the rack of coats, and flipped through them uncertainly, not really seeing them. She moved on to the counter where Edith kept scarves, evening bags, and gloves. Edith followed right on her heels. "Was there something else?" she said. It was obvious the woman wanted to get out of there but didn't quite know how. "Just looking," she said, smiling stupidly.

I recognized her accent, her clothes, and makeup. She was from Atlantic City, from a neighborhood like mine. If I'd come into Edith Clark's two years before, Edith would have treated me badly too, followed me around, watched my hands. Because I was married to John, people like Edith admired and trusted me. I didn't feel sorry for the girl from home, didn't care about her one way or the other. I watched her slip out the door and thought: That's not me anymore.

The very next time I went in, Edith made a bigger fuss over me than ever; she asked if I'd lost weight, said Lorraine had been in. She told John junior he was looking more like his daddy every day. I had to buy an evening dress for a fancy party a boyhood friend of John's was giving. I was nervous about going and so badly wanted to look elegant. I didn't know what I meant by that exactly, but I trusted that Edith would. "Of course, Mrs. Tyler," she said when I called ahead. "We'll find just the thing."

She had seven or eight dresses ready for me. Together we decided on an off-white chiffon. It was snug in the bust and hips, would have to be let out. Edith went off to get her tailor's chalk and pins from the back room, leaving me all alone.

I'd been so anxious about finding the right dress. With that done and Edith out of sight, I could relax. I felt exhilarated amidst all that finery.

SPLIT SKIRT

I picked up a pair of long white gloves, sniffed them, put them back on the counter. What was taking her so long? I began to get agitated—I had the dress, sure, but there was still the party to get through. What would I say to the other guests? Would John stay with me, or would he wander off? I felt the strain of being Mrs. Tyler to Edith's fawning Edith. One minute I was aware of the privilege of being left alone in a store; the next I was realizing I could steal something if I wanted to. I could take something from Edith, and she'd never be the wiser. But I'd have to hurry.

I grabbed a satin slip, folded it up, one, two, three, and tucked it under the mattress in John junior's carriage. When Edith returned five seconds later, I felt calm and confident. We disagreed about how the skirt of my new dress should fall, but I stood my ground. "Edith," I told her, "I want it just so."

Every single time I wore that slip—I wore it and wore it till it was frayed and soft as butter—I got a thrill, a boost, from the feel of it under my clothes.

My whole perspective shifts when I'm about to steal something. I suddenly realize the opportunity is right there in front of me. There'll be an inattentive clerk, or one who puts too much faith in who I seem to be, my expensive clothes, my charge cards. A crowded aisle can trigger it or even just a small item that feels especially good in my hand. I'm always terrified just before I do it. My pulse races, my toes curl inside my shoes. The theft itself I'm numb for; I mean, I'm so busy making it undetectable to the people around me. Once I've got what I want, I make a point of having a conversation with a saleswoman or another customer. I smile, I don't have any problem keeping up my end. Then I walk through the doors, terrified again, sure I'm about to be nabbed. Fifteen or twenty feet from the door, I take deep breaths of the outside air and feel the opposite of desperation—what, joy?

I try to explain this to doctors, but their eyes glaze over. They want to hear about my childhood, my adolescence.

Psychiatrists are great believers in order. It's all there for the figuring. No mystery is so dense that they can't get at its core, finally. They're either the last optimists or the most frightened people on earth, I can't decide which. They all want to know about the first time. I hate to tell a new one that I don't remember it. Margie and I used to shoplift when we were girls—hocking, we called it then. My mother would never let us have five cents, so we'd steal candy and gum from the drugstore. We knew the pharmacist, Mr. Mahoney, well. He used to ask after my mother, give her medicine on credit, that sort of thing. The women in the neighborhood went to him with their rashes and their kids' earaches and runny noses. For the price of the ointment or pills, they got some medical attention. If Margie and I had gotten caught, Mr. Mahoney would certainly have marched us right home to our mother.

After I stole from Edith, shoplifting became my secret hobby. I took note cards with fat little birds on them from a stationery store, cut-glass salt and pepper shakers from a gift shop. In the supermarket I'd stand at the checkout counter and slip boxes of Ludens cough drops into my purse. I liked to think that even if somebody watched me every second, he wouldn't see what I did.

Every so often dread would strike. I'd think about how awful it would be to get caught. John would be shocked and ashamed of me; he'd surely tell Lorraine. I knew there was something seriously wrong with me, believed I could cure myself if my will was strong enough. I decided I needed friends. All the time alone was making me peculiar. I wheeled the carriage over to the park near our house and smiled at every woman who looked my way.

SPLIT SKIRT

Never before in my life had I had to try to make friends. At home people just knew me. I was a Brennan, that's who I was. In the park I put women off, pelting them with questions. Where do you live, what does your husband do, how old is the baby? After a couple of minutes of that sort of thing, people get nervous. I'd wheel John junior home knowing I'd scared off another one. To ease the humiliation, I'd steal a little something.

Then new people moved in next door. Don't get your hopes up, I told myself, standing at my living room window and watching the moving van pull up to the curb. Their furniture was not what I'd come to think of as tasteful. It was a mishmash—a rose-colored satin chair with fringe, bunk beds, an old-fashioned breakfront. A tall woman with dark wavy hair supervised the moving men, walking alongside them smiling and gesturing emphatically. She looked stylish even in dungarees and sneakers, long and lean like a forties movie star, with full lips, white teeth, and good bones—distinctly Mediterranean. She wore a bright blue headband in her hair.

I waited a day, then knocked on her door. Women did that back then, paid formal welcome visits. You'd bring a cake or a bowl of potato salad, introduce yourself, give the newcomer advice about pediatricians and dry cleaners, tell her where the post office was. My new neighbor took her time answering the door. When she finally appeared, she looked at me, at the plate of raisin cookies in my hand, and said, "Oh, yeah, right. Come on in."

Her name was Judy Gennaro. Her living room was cluttered with boxes and God knows what. She cleared a place for me on the couch and told me she was from the south side of Philadelphia. Her husband Tom worked for Campbell Soup, had gotten a promotion and insisted they move out of the city. "So here we are," she said surveying the mess. She put the plate of cookies on a glass end table. As we talked, one of her daughters pulled back the wax paper, stacked four or five cookies on her palm and ran off with them. Judy watched without comment. I fought the impulse to put the plate out of reach in case the little girl came back for more.

I'd caught Judy in the middle of setting up her aquarium. "You mind if I work while we talk?" she said. I tried to tell her about the A&P and the Chinese laundry that did such a beautiful job on John's shirts, but she wasn't too interested. "Uh-huh," she said distractedly. "Look at this one," she said. "He's an angelfish." Her house was an absolute wreck, and she spent the afternoon opening bags of rainbow-colored gravel and releasing fish from baby-food jars.

The next morning I was out in the backyard hanging wash on the line. I didn't use the dryer except on days that were rainy or freezing cold. At first John objected to having a clothesline where people could see it, but he'd come to like the coarse feel of sheets and towels dried outside. I looked up and spotted Judy waving at me from a window. I waved back and felt a rush of relief. Finally somebody in that damn neighborhood liked me. Before I'd emptied my basket, Judy came outside, stood by the hedge between our yards, and said, "When you get finished there, how about showing me around?"

With John junior in his carriage and Judy's girls on foot, we headed out. Even the baby seemed to know this wasn't an ordinary day: He sat upright, hummed and drooled. Judy called him Fatso Prince, which stung a bit because of my weight, but it was apt, I had to admit. We went to the park and pushed Judy's girls on the swings. I liked knowing that other women were watching us. They couldn't help but notice Judy—her long strides, her loud laugh, her three dark-haired daughters. We ended our day at the soda fountain in the drugstore, where Judy drank black coffee and I hesitated, then ordered a chocolate ice cream soda.

Before long Judy had united the other women in the neighborhood, the same ones who'd snubbed me. She didn't belong any more than I did, but she made that seem exotic. Instead of their working on her, she worked on them. I began to notice other girls using Judy's expressions and gestures. She was always wanting to die or commit murder. Things she liked killed her. She put her thumb between her teeth and bit down hard when she concentrated. Judy wore black stretch pants while the rest of us were still wearing dresses. It wasn't long before some of the others started wearing those pants.

The incident that assured Judy's place as leader of the pack was the day she went out and bought a Cadillac without her husband. She and Tom had been car shopping for weeks but hadn't found what they were looking for. On her way to the grocery store one morning Judy stopped at a car lot, saw just the car she wanted, haggled over price, and bought it right there on the spot. She came home and paid whatever hell there was to pay—the whole neighborhood heard the shouting; goddamn Italians, John said—but Judy kept that car. The rest of us were awestruck. We'd sooner have gone off to Paris without our husbands' permission than buy a car, especially a Cadillac.

Judy and I became best friends. Of all the women in the neighborhood, she chose me. I'd never had a true best friend before. When I was younger I watched other girls pair off, exchange rings sometimes, make formal announcements of their best-friends status, but for me friendship had always been circumstantial. Socializing was an obligation, like going to school.

It was different with Judy. She and I spent part of every day together. We were privy to the most intimate details of each other's lives, and the most mundane. I knew her oldest daughter broke out in hives if she ate too much chocolate. She knew John and I had dinner with Lorraine every Wednesday night. Judy and I used to have a great time making fun of Lorraine. "How's her majesty, the royal queen of the United States?" Judy would ask on Thursday mornings.

The only thing Judy didn't know about me was that I was a thief. So many times I was tempted to tell her, after we'd spent a long summer afternoon talking or when she admitted something incriminating about herself. One day she told me she'd lied to her husband when they met, telling him she was two years younger than she really was. She'd been embarrassed about being twenty-four and unmarried. Tom didn't find out the truth until they were filling out the form for their marriage license. I didn't tell her I was a shoplifter because stealing was the one thing nobody knew about me and I wanted to keep it that way. I felt guilty for keeping a secret from Judy—we claimed to tell each other everything—but I justified that by reminding myself I didn't steal nearly as often as I used to. I didn't get the urge much once Judy came to town.

These were good years. Judy and I were at the center of a gang of half a dozen women. We all had houses and husbands and kids. We got pregnant and we delivered. I had David in '62, and Judy had another girl a year later. We all knew which of our marriages were good, tolerable, rotten. We were each other's coworkers. Our families were our jobs, and we talked a lot of shop.

We didn't socialize much as couples. We tried early on, but

things never quite got off the ground. When the men were around, my loyalties were divided. On the one hand, I hoped John wouldn't come off stodgy to Judy. On the other, I was afraid she'd seem brassy to him. And that wasn't all. I felt as if I were caught between two versions of myself. When I was with Judy, I felt smart and capable. She looked up to me, sought my advice. John is a good man, considerate and loving most of the time, but I often felt inept with him, frivolous. He told me what to do, interrupted me, rarely asked my opinion. Also, when it was just women, we talked about our husbands so much that when they were actually there in front of us, they cramped our style. Even Judy became circumspect in the presence of her husband.

Their marriage was not good. They used to have mean fights. I'd stand in my kitchen and listen to them shout. They fought about money—how little Tom made, how much Judy spent— and about the way Judy kept the house. I couldn't blame Tom there. Judy was a terrible slob. He thought she wasn't strict enough with the girls. Judy's daughters, though they were often grubby and wandered around on their own a good bit, were the brightest kids I knew, and they adored her. I'd walk into her house and find her lying on the floor playing Old Maid or dominoes with them.

One summer a town pool opened, Memorial Park. It was a manmade lake with a beach made of sand unloaded from the backs of trucks. Only residents were allowed to join, and that appealed to our snobbery. Judy and I would rush through our housework so we could get over there. She'd finish first, of course, then would come over and follow me around. When I defrosted my refrigerator or cleaned the oven, she watched with genuine curiosity. When I washed windows, she said, "Oh, come on." We'd pack our beach bags, fill Thermos jugs with Kool-Aid, round up our kids, and go.

Judy wore a two-piece bathing suit, very daring for those days. She had the figure—long legs, a nice round behind, you could wrap your two hands around her waist. She loved the water, did pikes off the high dive, swam out to the raft, then rubbed baby oil mixed with iodine on her skin and lay in the sun, one leg bent at the knee. Well, I hadn't slimmed down any, was still closer to a size fourteen than a twelve. My bathing suit was a flowered one-piece with a stiff bra built into it and a skirt that came to the middle of my thighs. I had to wear a stupid hat and one of John's T-shirts to keep from burning. Between Judy and me, we had six kids. While Judy was out playing water nymph, dark and sleek and, if you asked me, a little too familiar with several teenage boys, I got stuck standing in ankle-deep water watching the little guys dig in the sand.

When our husbands weren't home, Judy and I walked into each other's houses without knocking. So it happened that Judy caught me admiring a sweet little beach jacket I'd stolen from a lingerie shop. The kitchen door opened, and there she was. I jumped a foot, hid the jacket behind my back. "What've you got there," she said, "dirty pictures?" My heart was in my throat, and my hands shook as I held up the jacket for her to see. I tried desperately to act as if nothing was wrong, but it was the closest I'd ever come to getting caught, and it wasn't by a stranger in a store, it was Judy in my kitchen. I started to cry. "What?" Judy said, "Oh, honey, what's the matter?" Then her eyes narrowed. "Where'd you get that?"

I confessed, told her everything. She clapped her hand over her mouth and shook her head, but her eyes were bright and lively.

SPLIT SKIRT

In the end she kissed me and said she loved me for stashing booty in the baby carriage.

Judy thought my stealing was a riot. She didn't understand. She started stealing too, but not for kicks. Her husband was a terrible tightwad. He gave her twenty dollars a week for groceries, and whatever she could manage to hang on to from that was her spending money. She was always broke, used to borrow a dollar here, two there, forget to pay me back. Judy simply wanted things she didn't have the money to buy.

Because she was greedy, she wasn't a good shoplifter. Her movements were sudden and jerky. She'd look guilty walking *into* a store. Tom asked a lot of questions, and Judy had to make up complicated stories about where she'd gotten the new earrings, the perfume, the waterproof watch.

We got caught in Woolworth's, of all places. The manager stepped out in front of us as we tried to walk out, took hold of both our elbows, and escorted us and our kids to the back room. Judy had a package of emery boards down her pants. I had a big bag of M&M's in my purse. We begged the manager to let us pay for what we'd stolen, offered him double, triple, but he refused, called our husbands at work. "Mr. Tyler," he said gravely, "I have your wife and sons here."

John said his first thought was that I'd been kidnapped. He and Tom arrived together and had a private talk with the manager. We were let go. Out in the parking lot John insisted on putting the carriage in the backseat even though I asked him to let me walk it home. It was much too big to go in easily. John had a temper tantrum, forced it. When he does something like that, punches a wall or throws something, I always feel like I'm supposed to be grateful he's not taking his anger out on me, which is what he'd be doing but for his magnificent restraint. What I actually feel is disdain. I know he wouldn't do it at all if I weren't there to watch.

We pulled into our driveway just as Judy and Tom were getting out of their car. On the way into the house I tried to catch Judy's eye, but she wouldn't look at me. John told me to wait for him in the kitchen while he got the boys settled in the playroom.

I could hear Tom shouting, asking Judy where she'd gotten this or that—had she stolen them too? What the hell was the matter with her, was she crazy?

John came into the room and glared at me. "Would you mind telling me what this is all about?"

When I didn't answer, he got madder.

"You certainly don't have any trouble spending my money, so why in the hell would you steal a thirty-nine-cent bag of candy? The Tyler name means a lot in this—"

From next door came a crash. I heard Judy cry out.

I jumped up and pointed. "You go over there and make him stop that," I said.

John looked at me like I'd lost my mind. "I can't do that," he said, putting his hands on my shoulders and pressing down. "What goes on over there is none of our business."

I could have gone over there myself, but I didn't. I sat in my kitchen while next door my best friend got the daylights beaten out of her. My God, if a stranger had grabbed Judy on the street, I'd have kicked him in the groin, bit him, done whatever I could do. When her husband attacked her, I just sat there and listened.

TWENTY

*L*ights out. Can it be ten o'clock already? Mrs. Tyler rubs her hands together, clears her throat, brushes grit off her sheet. It's no cooler in here in the dark.

I lie down, turn on my side, pull my knees up. It's too hot to sleep, and this pillow smells like a musty dishrag. Is that Madeline snoring like an old man?

A couple of weeks ago my grandmother got sick. Her diabetes, her sugar, went haywire. She was miserable at home, complained constantly, took her illness ten times more seriously than anybody else did. Finally her doctor agreed to put her in the hospital. When I went to see her, she told me what she'd had for lunch, held the TV remote to my ear so I could hear how the sound came out of it, introduced me to her old-bat roommate, Josephine. As I got up to go, she nestled down in her bed, eyes bright.

"Rita is uncommunicative," a high school English teacher wrote in a letter to my parents. "She doesn't seem to like the reading lab or anything else." My parents were waiting for me when I got home. That letter was diagnosis and documentation. I wasn't a bad kid, hardly ever stayed out past my curfew, having, most nights, nowhere to go. I got decent grades and worked weekends at the ice cream parlor. The problem was my disposition. I was sullen, not morose so much as plain old unpleasant. "The whole world is out of step but you, is that it?" my mother shouted from the front door as I tore across the lawn in a fit of frustration and despair. All around me, it seemed, paths were narrowing, lights dimming.

I could have gone to college right after high school but didn't; I refused to toe the line. I was rebellious in a brainless, backfirey way. Instead of going to college, I got a better waitressing job and moved into an apartment with my sister Eva.

We became part of a community of people on no particular track. We all worked menial jobs, went out to bars and parties five or six nights a week, didn't think or talk about the future. For those of us uneasy in limbo there was a halfhearted sense of a counterculture. A poster on the wall of a house five or six guys shared showed the top of a man's head being unscrewed, his skull filled with sand, a college degree awarded.

Down deep, I think, I wanted somebody to pull me aside and say, "Rita, honey, you're too smart to be a waitress and spend your nights drinking in bars." If anybody had tried it, I would have rolled my eyes, said leave me alone, I hate you.

Bar owners and local drug dealers and boys we'd gone to high school with climbed the rickety stairs to our apartment carrying cases of beer and hibachis and bongs in brown paper bags. Some mornings Eva and I would meet at the refrigerator, look each other in the eye, and say, "Get rid of him." Once we were alone, we'd sit out on the fire escape and tell stories about our adventures.

I saved up five hundred dollars, got dealer financing, bought a used two-seater convertible, bright red with a hard top. Eva and I thought we were very beautiful riding around in that car—when we could get it started. It was temperamental as hell. Mechanics would grimace when they looked under the hood and saw oil-soaked electrical tape, hoses attached on one end only, clumps of gnarled wire.

I was driving to work one afternoon when all of a sudden steam hissed out of the floor on the passenger side. It's lucky Eva wasn't sitting there or she'd have gotten her feet scalded. I pulled over and went through the usual routine, a telephone call, a tow truck. The battery had sprung a leak. That was acid spewing into the passenger compartment. I bought a new battery but didn't do a very thorough job cleaning up the original explosion. The battery acid I left behind ate through the carpet, making the whole car smell like burned fur.

A thirty-year-old hippie, an elder in our group, threw a big Fourth of July party one year; there were hundreds of people in a field, kegs of beer, local bar bands. A boy from high school, a handsome track star home from college, was there without his blond girlfriend. He and I had been pals in grade school but had barely spoken since. In the sixth grade we'd eaten lunch together every day, both owned blue-and-red striped T-shirts and would agree to wear them on certain days so we'd match—squirrelly prepubescent stuff like that. In high school we'd gone in very different directions. He was clean-cut college bound; I spent most of my time smoking dope in the parking lot. At the party he sat down beside me and we talked, awkwardly at first but with increasing animation. We discovered we still liked each other the way we had as kids. By nightfall we'd wandered off and were kissing under a tree.

I remember the desire I'd feel after making out with a boy for an hour or so—lust and anxiety. Was I going to be with him? *With* with was how Eva and I said it. I'd want to but would feel anticipatory remorse. At the Fourth of July party the day had been clear and dry, the night cool and inviting. I decided only the virulent cliquishness of high school had kept this boy and me apart.

He'd ridden his bicycle to the party, this wholesome boy, so he gave me directions to his house. I knew where he lived but didn't let on. His parents were in Europe, had been gone a couple of weeks already. The kitchen was messy and welcoming. After spending so much time in the cheap apartments of my friends, I found his house roomy and plush. He carried me up the stairs, straining a bit—he was track and field, not football—but we made it. His room had a narrow twin bed and trophies and smelled like sneakers.

He put me down on the bed, kissed me, and before long we were helping each other out of our clothes. I wasn't wearing any underwear; going without made me feel licentious and strong-willed, defiant. This boy jumped when he slipped his hand into my jeans. He gasped—just the response I was after.

In the morning we stood by my sports car. He admired it until he stuck his head inside and saw the wound from the battery acid. By this time the metal under the carpet had started to go. The car smelled the way I imagine a nuclear reactor might. He stepped back and said his girlfriend wouldn't be home for another two days. Would I come over again that night? Sure, I said.

SPLIT SKIRT

No way, I thought. I knew I'd be soaking in a hot tub, trying to figure out how to tell Eva a funny story about my night with a jock.

A few months later I got pregnant by the older man I told you about before, had my abortion, lost heart. I'd been getting drunk too often, even blacked out a couple of times. One night I was sitting in a bar watching boys play pool when I decided I'd rather be home. I was driving down the highway when my convertible's hard top blew clear off. I felt a rush of frigid air, and I gasped, thinking a door had swung open, until I looked up and saw the moon, full and white and reproachful. What does God have to do, I asked myself, knock on your damn door? I pulled over and walked a quarter of a mile before I spotted the car's roof leaning up against the divider. I dodged cars and eighteen-wheelers to retrieve it. Lugging that thing back, I knew I couldn't keep up the appearance of reckless disregard much longer.

Eva had been attending a local college for a year or so. She noticed the dip in my spirits and convinced me to sign up for a class, which I did squeamishly. Trouble finding a parking space or a long line at the bursar's office would make me want to bolt. Then, in my freshman composition class, I discovered literature. I became an English major, joined a circle of middle-aged housewives and divorced mothers—nontraditional students, the administration called us. Oh, were we earnest. We spent hours on the phone and in the cafeteria discussing books and professors, husbands and mothers and kids. I liked these women because they were smart but not ethereal, firmly rooted in the physical world. They'd talk about *The Odyssey* one minute, a sale at Mandee's the next.

Working and going to school, I didn't have the time or energy to go out much at night. I spent most of my free time alone, would tell Eva to say I wasn't home when any of the guys I used to go out with called for me. Months passed, and then it was a year since I'd had sex. I didn't think about it much, but every once in a while I'd get a panicky sense of acute isolation. Skin hunger, I guess it was. I felt like I was going to get sick and maybe die if somebody didn't touch me soon. One of my nephews turned five, and we had a birthday party for him. A timid kid, he was overwhelmed by the fuss. In the middle of opening a mountain of presents, he crawled onto my lap, put his head on my chest, and sucked his fingers. What a relief it was to hold him, to smell his skin and feel his hard shoe bang against my shin.

Just before I met Alex, I went on a date with a guy I met at work. He arrived on a Harley Davidson and took me for a tortuous ride up in the mountains. Not once during the entire date did he call me by my name. He kept calling me Lady. I was writing a paper on *The Turn of the Screw,* had discovered conclusive evidence that the ghosts aren't real, so the governess must be crazy, couldn't wait to get home to my Highlighter and my feverish notes. When the date was finally over, I ran up the stairs to my apartment, sore from the motorcycle, half-deaf from its roar. Closing the door behind me, I made up my mind to go on for a master's degree, then a Ph.D. I'd become a secular nun.

The first time I saw Alex he was looking at me. He was tall, with broad shoulders and green eyes. There was a stillness about him, a sense that he'd been chastened. His gaze wasn't predatory, but it was forceful.

I was sitting at a table in a bar with a couple of girlfriends and Eva. They were gearing up for a big night, I was thinking about going home. Alex's good looks convinced me to stay. I got up and went to the bar. Alex smiled and said, "You don't mess around." He bought me a drink. Our conversation wasn't exactly effortless—I was nervous, a handsome older man in a business suit drinking scotch and water, oh, boy—but it wasn't stilted small talk either. There was that boiled-down essence of fun you feel when you finally find somebody you like.

He'd just moved out of the house he'd shared with Lee and was renting a studio apartment not far from where I lived. It was July, muggy and still. His apartment had no air conditioner, a mattress on the floor, mismatched sheets. We didn't do a lot of talking once we got there. I was distracted by his lips, couldn't wait to kiss him.

When Alex touched me, it was as if I'd taken a drug that erased the memory of every awkward sexual experience, every demeaning one. He kissed my neck and current ran all the way down to my toes. It felt so much better than it ever had before, as if all five senses and their separate abilities to perceive pleasure merged. I didn't know it then, but it had been a long time for Alex too. We both had skin hunger.

Before we fell asleep, Alex got up and went to the bathroom. I heard the sound of fabric ripping. He came back to bed with a piece of towel, cool and wet. We'd sweated rivers by then. He washed my face, my chest, down my stomach, between my legs. He was gentle but thorough, attentive to folds and creases.

The next morning we woke up naked and shy, found our underwear in a hurry. Alex made coffee, and we talked about his situation and mine. He told me he'd just split with his wife, wouldn't be divorced for a year, had two kids. I was vague—no, I lied. I said I was seeing somebody but it wasn't serious, because I didn't want him to think I was undesirable. He gave me a pencil and a paper towel and told me to write down my phone number.

I was sure I'd hear from him right away. Two days passed,

three, four, and I'm cursing myself for expecting otherwise. I was just like the girls I couldn't stand listening to, the ones who slept with men and then expected their lives to change.

I went to a party at the house of a woman I worked with. Her husband had been coming on to me for months. I flirted up a storm with him that night because Alex hadn't called. The party dwindled down. Finally it was just the three of us—Linda, hubby, me. Linda started yawning, said good night, and left me alone with her husband, who pulled me onto his lap. After ten minutes of soggy kissing, he started making noises about my joining Linda and him in bed. The whole thing was a setup. "Linda's waiting for us," he said in a croaky voice that sprayed spit in my ear.

What kind of girl did he think I was? He was barely attractive, and Linda was a string bean with no sense of humor. I ran out of there and cried all the way home, convinced I was a freak of a person who only bad things would ever happen to.

Alex was sitting on my stoop when I pulled up. "I'm sorry," he said as I got out of the car. He was apologizing for not calling and for waiting by my door in the middle of the night, but in my hysteria I lost sight of logic and assumed he was sorry about the creepy couple who'd tried to lure me into their bed and about my feeling like I had two heads. I fell into his arms. He told me he hadn't called because he'd vowed he was going to spend at least one year alone after his marriage came apart. It was getting light when we went inside, brushed our teeth, and climbed into bed. A month later Eva moved out and Alex moved in.

We didn't go out much at night except to the movies or to dinner by ourselves. Alex's friends were old and married, mine were young and used drugs. The few times I did go out by myself to see my old friends, I was bored. I missed Alex and wished I was lying next to him on our couch, reading while he watched sports on TV or did paperwork. When I got home, even if it was only ten or eleven o'clock, Alex would be sullen. He wanted me to stay home at night with him, period. I'd dote on him, coax him out of his snit.

Every once in a while, early on, our sudden intimacy would scare me. I'd balk, revert to my tough-cookie ways. Alex had to be patient. Once he dropped me off at work and said he couldn't wait until I got home, said it simply, without sap. "Don't be such a jerk," I said, jumped out of the car, slammed the door. When I got home that night, I swallowed hard and apologized. "How'd you get so mean?" he said.

For as long as I could remember I'd been dead set against being what anybody might consider soft. Oh yeah? I walked around thinking, oh yeah? All of a sudden, with Alex, I was trying to be a kind and loving woman. I wanted to be that for him, I really did, but every so often I'd fall way short of the mark.

Alex had his own reasons for diving into our relationship so eagerly. The breakup of his marriage had left him raw. He hadn't seen it coming, at least that's what he said. Lee had had an affair, fallen in love, and left him. For Alex, divorce was a personal failure. He'd loved this woman and lost her, had been unable to convince her to stay married to him. His children's lives had been disrupted. Kevin started having nightmares, so Lee took him to a psychologist, who diagnosed depression. I came home and found Alex in an altered state—flushed, pacing, his eyes bright and jumpy. "A seven-year-old depressed," he said. "Where does he go from here?"

I was with Alex whenever I wasn't at work or school. If we didn't shower together, one would sit on the toilet and keep the other company. When I went shopping, Alex sat in that chair outside the dressing room, that husband chair, and helped me decide what to buy. He jogged in the evening, so I did too. Eva asked if she would ever again see me without him. "I like Alex," she said, "but come on."

I never felt as surely and plainly myself as I did in Alex's presence. It was as if something that had been rattling around inside me found its place. The rest of the time I had to decide how to act, what to say, how to seem. A paralyzing self-consciousness undermined me. Once I got comfortable with Alex, I didn't try to be anything, I just was. Riding along in the car or fixing dinner while he sat at the kitchen table, I'd close my eyes so I could better feel how easy it was to be with him. One afternoon he trimmed my hair. I sat still while he worked his way around. I felt like a girl in a perfect world, the tilt of my head, Alex's absolute attention, his breath in my ear, then on my neck and shoulders.

Our love wasn't rich like the food in an expensive restaurant: it was good soup on a cold night. When I woke up in the morning and there was Alex, waking up too, I'd marvel at my good fortune. Men are most appealing in the morning, when they're sleepy, boyish, before they get their egos on straight. It must have to do with survival of the species. Nature knows she better make men soft and sweet at some point during the day if she expects women to continue having sex with them. I'll bet a lot of forgiving goes on in the morning. One of my sisters is a scientist who does research on early childhood. She says babies and toddlers are adorable because they have to be. Nobody would put up with them otherwise. Think about the way old people get treated. Maybe if they were a little cuter, people would be nicer to them.

For about a year Alex and I flopped around this way, nuzzling and trading secrets. Then one night he came to pick me up at work. He sat at the bar and watched me wait on a table of businessmen. One of them, a big florid guy, kept teasing me, wanted me to order for him, that sort of thing. Some men believe what they're paying for in a restaurant is the waitress's womanly attention. You don't wait on them so much as date them for an hour. I was humoring this joker, working on a fat tip. When I went to the bar for drinks, Alex said, "What's that big guy's problem?" I was tired and didn't like the tone of Alex's voice. I shrugged. "Just another asshole."

In the car on the way home, Alex said he wanted me to quit my job. The work was demeaning; I shouldn't have to put up with jerks showing off for their friends. I argued because I thought I should; I said tips were good and we needed the money—a little jab there—Alex's obligations to Lee and the kids ate up half his salary. He got furious, sped through intersections, raced around curbs, stopped hard in front of our building.

Alex's anger was evidence of his commitment to me, his taking responsibility for me. It felt good. Some part of me luxuriated in it. I wanted to find a different sort of job but knew nothing else I might do would pay as well as restaurant work. Since Alex and I split the rent and other household bills fifty-fifty, I thought I had to keep bringing in a certain amount of money even though waitressing was taking its toll on me. When I approached a new table or stood waiting for an indecisive customer to order, I had to ride out a wave of irritation so potent it made my face perspire. Waitresses have a joke: When a man orders for a woman and says, "The lady will have . . . ," a waitress thinks, "And the slut will go get it."

I found a part-time job in an insurance agency. The work was boring, and I earned less than half of what I'd made waiting tables, but Alex said I shouldn't worry about the money, I should concentrate on getting my degree. I'd never worked in an office before, and I liked wearing skirts and pumps, having a desk, a typewriter, a bottom drawer full of supplies. My boss was a nervous little guy who was always looking over my shoulder and catching mistakes. He used to tell me how hard it was for him to meet girls. When he found out I have seven sisters, he begged me to set him up with one. Coincidentally, he had the same name as a boy I'd gone to high school with, a real good-looking guy, a heartbreaker. I got a big charge out of that, the new Bob Allen compared to the old.

Alex and I were eating dinner in a Chinese restaurant one night. I was in the middle of a story about Bob when Alex threw down his chopsticks and said he didn't want to hear it. Why did I talk about this guy so much? What was going on between us? Bob Allen was a wimp, I said, far from the sort of man I'd have an affair with if I was going to have an affair. "So you'd cheat," he said, "just not with this guy?" On and on it went. Alex and I didn't speak to each other for three days. Finally he came home with a dozen red roses, apologized, and asked me to marry him.

I was caught off guard but happily so. Alex wasn't yet divorced, and we had never discussed marriage in so many words. We talked about the future, about my going to graduate school locally, about buying a house, but we'd always talked around our getting married. The next day we went out and bought a diamond engagement ring. I liked showing it off to people—my sisters, the women in my classes—but when I was alone, I used to look down at my diamond and say out loud, "Whose hand is that?"

A couple of months later I was on my way to my car in the college parking lot when I saw one of my women friends leaning against the bumper of her car, smoking a cigarette. I hadn't seen her in a while; once Alex and I got together I didn't spend much time in the college cafeteria or on the telephone, so I wasn't really part of the ladies' club anymore. I asked her what was up. She'd gotten a C on a Shakespeare midterm and was in tears. We went across the street to a bar, had a couple of beers, and gossiped about the professor. I was glad to be out with another woman, this woman in particular. She was brilliant and eccentric, had a husband and four kids, wrote beautifully, and nothing I said ever shocked her. When I got home three hours late, Alex accused me of having something going with somebody at school.

After every fight I'd convince myself that Alex's love was worth an occasional bout of jealousy, that his believing so many men were after me every second of the day was evidence of his devotion.

On the morning Alex's divorce was final, he and I went out to breakfast. The mood was supposed to be celebratory, and he tried. He kept saying he was happy, but there wasn't much color in his face. To be expected, I told myself, the end of a ten-year marriage. Who wouldn't tremble?

He wanted us to get married right away. "We'll do it after I graduate," I said. "One thing at a time."

I've always maintained that Alex's jealousy was irrational, his problem entirely. Here I might as well admit I wasn't as innocent as I always claimed to be. Whenever I came across an attractive man in one of my classes or at work, I'd try to get his attention, and I'd succeed some of the time. Nothing ever came of any of it. Maybe I'd get asked out and act surprised: I'm sorry, I thought you knew I live with my boyfriend. I even did it with old Bob at the insurance office. With him I engaged in an ancient feminine pastime: a woman declares a man undesirable, a good pal, then gets off on flirting with him—bending over when he just happens to be nearby, telling him juicy tidbits about her personal life, crossing her legs and watching his eyes. Bob looked at me like I was famous. He was star-struck.

Agnes Rossi

You know what the God's honest truth is? I don't know how to relate to men except as men, sexually, romantically, hunter/huntedly. I believe I'm supposed to flirt with all of them.

As Alex got more and more difficult, my understanding of myself as a sensible girl involved with a jealous man became dear to me. My rational self understood that Alex's jealousy was a serious problem—he insisted I wear slips, the outline of my thighs through a skirt enraged him. A sane girl would have to consider leaving him, and I did, constantly. I didn't go because Alex warmed some part of me that had been chilled through and through for so long. I used to imagine something small and bony like an eaglet frozen in murky brown ice. The sun comes out, the temperature rises. This thing, whatever it is, creaks, cracks, comes to life. Nobody had ever looked at me the way Alex did.

After my grandmother was in the hospital for a couple of days, the doctors did some horrible test on her, put a tube down her throat. They couldn't sedate her or it wouldn't work. The poor thing had to gag her way through it. I saw her just afterward. She couldn't talk, and her face was tear-stained. She pulled the sheet up to her chin, turned away.

I married Alex one week after my college graduation. While the wedding plans were under way, I spent a lot of time at my mother's house. She and I decided who to invite, what colors my sisters should wear, made up the seating chart, all that stuff. I'd look up from whatever we were doing, realize it was late, call Alex and tell him I was going to spend the night because my mother and I had fifty things to do yet. Alex stayed out of the planning as much as he could; he was sweet and funny about it, said I should be sure to let him know the time and place, and tell him what to wear.

SPLIT SKIRT

I was very busy and very nervous—ordinary jitters, everybody said, but I knew it was more than that. There was a steady ache in the pit of my stomach. I think some part of me believed I was making a mistake—my hands shook constantly—but there were flowers to order, travel brochures to compare. I had a bizarre but powerful desire to move back into my parents' house; I hated to leave there. I hung out with my mother even when there was nothing left to do.

The night before the wedding my system went haywire. The ache in my stomach intensified, turning sharp and hot. My mother eyed me nervously, kept telling me to settle down. I said good night to Alex in the parking lot of the restaurant where we'd had the rehearsal dinner—we'd agreed to sleep apart that night. As soon as he pulled away I convinced Eva and two of my younger sisters to take me out to one of our old haunts. Driving to the bar, I got teary looking at Eva's profile. I remember staring up at the night sky. The face on the moon has always looked shocked and horrified to me, like it's looking down at the earth saying Ohmigod!

It was a Friday night, and the bar was jumping. I drank too much, talked to strange men, made an ass of myself. I saw condemnation in the eyes of the wildest of my old friends. Even barflies, it turns out, know that on the night before her wedding a bride should be in bed. Eva pulled me into the bathroom at one point and said, "Rita, you don't have to go through with this wedding if you don't want to." We were silent for five or ten seconds, a terrifying moment of truth, but I ducked out of it, told her I was fine, just having a last hurrah for myself. "Lighten up, Eva," I said.

I vaguely remember stumbling into my parents' house. My mother was waiting for us. I was seeing double, two of my mother, furious, hair in curlers, face slick with night cream. I expected her to yell, but she was too angry even for that. She just glared at me. "Alex called three times," she said finally. "I suggest you call him before you pass out." I went into the kitchen, picked up the phone, dialed my mother's number, pulled the receiver into the dining room, and closed the door.

The next morning I could barely lift my head off the pillow. My sisters huddled around, a couple climbed into bed with me, the ones who'd been out too. The others, the married sisters, brought us aspirin and juice and mugs of icy ginger ale. What I had was no ordinary hangover—it was like a combination of the flu and a prolonged anxiety attack. My parents stood over me like great scowling statues. Here they'd spent all this money on a wedding, and not only am I marrying a divorced man—a tribunal had to grant us permission to have a church service—but I'm lying in bed like a lummox after my mother has ordered me up three separate times.

My sisters did what they could, made me take a shower and brush my teeth, curled my hair, put makeup on me. The second they'd leave me unattended, I'd go back to bed. It was spooky, seeing all seven of my sisters wearing identical rose-colored dresses. They looked like some weird female army, dolled up for battle. Finally my dress was zipped and buttoned and snapped, the veil was bobby-pinned in place, and I limped out to the limo.

Alex turned and narrowed his eyes as my father and I made our way down the aisle. Despite my sisters' best efforts, I looked like the bride in *Night of the Living Dead.*

Adrenaline or something intervened at the altar, and I made it through the ceremony. I remember Alex holding my right hand and Eva my left; the priest had the kindest blue eyes. Our recessional music was the standard end-of-wedding tune, the one that they used to use at the beginning of *The Newlywed Game*—remember that? Dun, dun, da-dun-dun-dun-dun. It was wild to hear it for real, to be the bride heading away from the altar while that thing rang out. In the back of the church Alex and I stood with our parents as the guests filed past. I started to feel dizzy again, was afraid I was going to pass out or worse. I told Alex I'd be right back, broke away from the pack of well-wishers, went and stretched out on the backseat of the limo, sweating, swallowing, trying to keep all that damn tulle flat so nobody would spot me.

The reception wasn't much better. "Where the heck is the bride?" guests started asking. I spent as much time as I could in a little changing room the hotel provided for the bridal party. My grandmother got wise to me, came in after me and said people were beginning to talk. Her sisters, my ancient great aunts, were going around saying I had morning sickness, which wasn't very inventive of them, considering Alex and I had been living to-gether for over a year and everybody knew it. My grandmother rubbed one of my hands between her two and said, "You're going out there now, dolly, and dance with your father, cut the cake, throw your bouquet. Come on," she said, "we'll go to-gether."

Alex was a groom and a half. He had to be. He kissed every-body, danced every dance, went around with the white silk bag collecting envelopes with money in them. Once we were alone in our hotel room, he collapsed in a chair.

I was lying on the bed in full regalia, had forgotten to change into my pale-blue leaving suit, couldn't have told you where it was, even. We were silent for ten or fifteen seconds, and then Alex said, "What is wrong with you, Rita? You wait your whole life for this day, spend six months planning it, then go out and get drunk the night before?"

I apologized, of course, said I didn't know what had come over me. I'm a fuckup, I said, I fuck everything up. He rolled his eyes, then took off his jacket, bow tie, and cummerbund. He lay down beside me and put his arm around my waist. We both fell right to sleep. A few hours later I woke up, wrestled myself out of my dress, took a hot bath, and climbed into bed. But I couldn't go back to sleep. I would have given anything to undo the last twenty-four hours, to be back in the parking lot after the rehearsal dinner. Alex looked so sweet, sound asleep on top of the covers, still wearing his tuxedo pants and shirt. I covered him with the bedspread and swore I'd make it up to him. I'd been a lousy bride, but I'd be a perfect wife. I felt lucky to have him.

My wedding pictures are a disgrace. I'm pale and hunched over. My eyes are bloodshot, my mascara smeared, my veil cockeyed. My headpiece wouldn't stay on—the damn thing kept slithering down my back. Now, at least, my wedding will be jettisoned out of the universe of the sacred. I can stop feeling guilty about ruining it.

A couple of months ago I went to Atlantic City with my grandmother. On the bus I tried for the first time to make a joke about what a disaster I'd been as a bride.

"Look at it this way," I said. "You have so many granddaughters. Some have been better brides before me, others will be better brides after me. One dud out of eight isn't so bad."

She started to laugh, really laugh; her shoulders jiggled and she put her hand on my knee. I could tell she was remembering what a mess I'd been, could see me sitting on the couch in that little room mopping my brow. I was so relieved, thinking she was with me. But then she straightened up in her seat and wiped the smile off her face.

"Don't make fun, Rita," she said. "Don't you dare. You should be ashamed of the way you carried on. I don't know why that husband of yours puts up with you."

My grandmother understood perfectly well why a person

might sabotage her own wedding, I know she did, but she couldn't let on. It's her duty as an elder to come down squarely on the side of propriety. When I get out of here, I'm going over to see her. I'm going to remind her about when she was sick and scared at home, how safe she felt at first when her doctor admitted her to the hospital, how she thought she had it made, until they put a tube down her throat.

TWENTY-ONE

*A*ndrew, my third son, was just two when John decided it was time for us to move. The house Lorraine had given us for a wedding present was fine for a starter, but John was doing well and we could afford much better. I was dead set against leaving Ventnor at first—my friends were there, John junior and David were in school. But I had to be practical; our house had only three bedrooms, and I planned to have another baby, try once more for a girl.

By this time the bulk of the family business had shifted to New York. John spent two or three days there every week, and had hired a driver so he could make use of the time on the road. He wanted us to live within commuting distance of Manhattan. Lorraine scouted around and chose Saddle River, New Jersey.

She was certain the real estate there would one day be worth ten times what we'd pay for it, and of course, she was right.

John was too busy to house-hunt, so he decided Lorraine and I should do it. I dreaded spending time alone with her, couldn't imagine what we'd find to talk about. We hadn't been in each other's company without John and the boys since the morning years earlier when she'd tried to bully me out of my marriage. I have to say I'd been amazed by Lorraine's willingness to put all of that behind her. Where I come from, if a mother-in-law and a daughter-in-law battled the way we had, they'd never speak again, not civilly, anyway. When the time came, the daughter-in-law would sit stony-faced at the old lady's funeral. Lorraine was something else. She acted as if she and I had been involved in a negotiation that got messy for a while but was over. She was a practical woman. John was her son and I was his wife and let's get on with it. I believe she liked me better for standing my ground, the way one businessman might have a grudging respect for another who drove a hard bargain.

It turns out we did just fine, Lorraine and I. We house-hunted two or three days every week. I'd get up in the morning, put on good clothes, and drive to Atlantic City to pick up my mother, who'd volunteered to babysit. She'd been temporarily laid off, and she was eager to help out, to spend some time alone with her grandsons. John wanted me to slip her some money, but she wouldn't take it. She gave me one of her looks—get off your high horse—when I offered it.

My mother was stern with the boys but not forbidding, exactly the way her mother had always been with me. Irish grandmothers don't go in for a lot of spoiling. They treat children with a kind of austere familiarity. Time with my mother did my kids good. With Grandma Brennan they discovered the whole world wasn't theirs for the asking.

186

SPLIT SKIRT

Lorraine and I would head up the Garden State Parkway in her dark blue Jaguar. Saddle River was still pretty rural in 1969. So green, working farms and vegetable stands on the side of the road. It all made a me little queasy, seemed very far from home. I was so grateful for Lorraine's energy. You should have seen her. She rode up front with the real estate agent, sat ramrod straight, alert by instinct like a hunting dog, listening to an inner voice that said buy, buy, buy. She carried a leather-bound notebook, jotted down addresses, features, and figures, tapped a pen against her front teeth when an agent gave her a sales pitch.

My reluctance to move evaporated when I saw what I'd get in the bargain. A long driveway, woods, an enormous kitchen with a dishwasher, a bedroom for each of my kids plus a couple of extras for guests. I was seduced by cathedral ceilings, Oriental rugs, grandfather clocks. When Lorraine left me alone in a formal dining room with a chandelier or at the entrance to a long, long hallway, I'd look around and think, Not bad for a girl from Atlantic Avenue. Not bad at all.

At the end of each day Lorraine and I would stop at the Paramus Diner and review the day's houses over cheeseburger platters. It would be dusk when we went in, dark when we came out. High on coffee, we'd head home.

My mother and John would be sitting in the den watching TV together. I'd look in on the boys. They'd be sound asleep, clean and fed, their rooms tidy, their clothes laid out on their dressers for the next day. John, Lorraine, my mother, and I would have a cup of tea and fill each other in on our days. It was good, fortifying, sitting at the kitchen table with our mothers, keeping our voices down because our sons, their grandsons, were asleep upstairs.

Lorraine always gave my mother a lift home. John and I would walk them out to the driveway, and watch them pull away in

Lorraine's fancy car. Our mothers weren't as different as I'd once thought. They'd both worked hard all their lives, were domineering, took good care of the people they loved. John said they didn't so much get along as they recognized and approved of each other. After they left, John and I would lie in bed and laugh, wondering what in the world our mothers found to talk about between Ventnor and Atlantic City.

Lorraine and I must've looked at fifty houses before we found ours. Eleven acres, woods in front and behind, eight bedrooms, five baths, a built-in swimming pool, and a barn. The owners were divorcing and eager to sell. Lorraine negotiated brilliantly. We moved as soon as school let out.

It was easier than it should have been to leave my friend Judy. The day after we got caught stealing in Woolworth's, I'd waited until our husbands left for work, then went over to see her. She had a fat lip and a black eye. There were bruises up and down her arms. "What are you going to do?" I said, my voice conspiratorial and urgent, as if Judy's beating were just the latest intrigue on the block. Judy looked at me disdainfully, then turned away. *"Do?"* she said. "What do you think I'm going to do?"

Judy couldn't hide her bruises, not in that neighborhood. It was humiliating for her and demoralizing for the rest of us. She had to wear sunglasses in the supermarket.

She started keeping to herself. Days would go by and I wouldn't see her. We stopped walking into each other's houses without knocking. We talked only about our kids; I never asked her how things were going with Tom.

Judy's marriage deteriorated steadily. Raised voices and slamming doors would wake me up at all hours. One night I looked out my window and saw a police car in Judy's driveway. I believe Judy withdrew from our friendship because she was proud. Her situation—continuing to live with a man who beat her—elicited pity. It was easier for her to go it alone.

I didn't press, told myself Judy had a right to her privacy, to manage her trouble her own way. The truth is, I was grateful not to know what was going on next door. I didn't want Judy to confide in me. There was something crude and vulgar about a man hitting his wife. I'd left that sort of ugliness behind me on Atlantic Avenue. My own husband had hit me once, but some-how that didn't figure in my thinking. I came to believe a differ-ent sort of woman would be a more appropriate friend for me, somebody whose husband made as much money as John, some-body classier, more refined.

One morning as Lorraine and I were pulling out to go house-hunting, I saw Judy sitting on the porch of her house, her feet up on the railing. I waved; she brought her coffee cup to her lips, looked away.

The day before we moved, Judy came over to say goodbye. She cried, but I didn't. Let's face it, I couldn't have Judy *and* the eleven acres, the French doors, the oak-paneled study for my husband.

Saddle River was as different from Ventnor as Ventnor had been from Atlantic City. In Ventnor our houses had been relatively small and close together. We women were in each other's busi-ness. If somebody's kids were sick or her furnace gave out in the dead of winter, everybody knew it. But in Saddle River I could barely glimpse the closest house from my front porch. There was privacy, to be sure, but there was also isolation. Everybody was older, too; we were all less willing to complicate our lives by getting to know neighbors.

John didn't want me to hire a housekeeper at first. He'd grown up with a series of maids and cleaning ladies but had gotten accustomed to living without them and didn't want a stranger in the house. With three boys under ten and a house the size of a small hotel, I never worked so hard in my life. My shift started at six in the morning and ran straight through until eleven at night.

John was exacting, wanted things just so. Once I overheard him tell a couple of men at a cocktail party that he ran a tight ship at home. He was perched on the arm of a chair, expounding on the order of things. He made me sick. I'd show him, I decided; I'd walk out, take the car and leave him there. I got as far as the driveway before I realized I didn't have the keys. I was not too far from home, just a mile or two, but it was cold out, and besides, I was wearing high heels. What was I going to do, go inside and ask my husband for the keys, then storm out a second time? I tried the front door, but it was locked, so I went around to the back and snuck in through the kitchen.

In the car on the way home I told John I hadn't appreciated his comment about the tight ship. "Just talk," he said. "Where were you, anyway? I didn't see you." I told him I wanted a housekeeper. If we can afford five bathrooms, I said, we can damn well afford somebody to clean them.

"We have somebody," he said. "We have you."

I didn't say another word to him for the rest of the evening. I slept in one of the guest rooms. The next morning I called a domestic employment agency from the telephone in the kitchen while John was making his own coffee. I hired the first applicant they sent over. "John," I said when he got home that evening, "this is Catherine."

"Hullo there," he said. "Nice to meet you."

We started entertaining a lot, John's business associates and their wives mostly. Catherine and I would spend days getting ready; unfortunately, the preparations were the best part. The dinners themselves were a big bore. The only point of the conversation so far as I could see was for us all to get from one moment to the next as smoothly as possible. People didn't tell stories; they asked polite questions and got predictable answers. Nobody ever said, You'll never believe what happened to me yesterday. Our guests were refined, it was true. A lot had been filtered out of them.

I read that the queen of England can make small talk with anybody. When she has her portrait painted, she keeps the pleasantries going for hours at a time without ever compromising the royal privacy. She'd have been a big hit at one of our parties.

I'd plan a lovely menu, order flowers, spend hours dressing, then sit there smiling nervously, waiting for the fun to start. An hour into it I'd wish I could sneak off and take a hot bath.

It was my fault as much as anybody's. These people had polish, and I was intimidated. I talked too much or not at all, couldn't find the groove, learn the language. My discomfort was contagious. I regularly jammed up the works at my end of the table.

I believed I was letting John down. He needed and deserved a wife who knew how to conduct herself. I'd look at other women and think, there now, she'd be a good wife for John. Miss Size Six over there—they were all so damn thin—she'd be perfect. Because of the business relationships involved, the men were often vying for John's attention, and their wives, doing their part, fawned over him as well. I'd watch John being charmed by a smoothie and wonder if he was comparing me to her.

Sometimes I'd become a kind of caricature of myself, play up my humble origins. I'd hear myself putting on the Atlantic City in my voice, mentioning that my father had been a bartender, that I hadn't gone to college, that I'd never been to Europe. Since I clearly wasn't making it as one of them, I thought I might be valued for my quaint working-class color.

One evening I drank too much wine in an effort to relax. My speech slurred a little at dinner, and I was embarrassed; I drank too much coffee then, trying to sober up. After everybody left I couldn't sleep, so I got out of bed and went down to the kitchen. I felt awful, the wine and the coffee, my nerves. Why were these evenings so hard for me? Why did I make such a big deal out of something that should have been easy?

John came into the kitchen, tying the sash of his bathrobe and squinting in the light. I told him I was sorry I wasn't a more graceful hostess, that I wasn't like the woman I'd seen him talking to for nearly an hour in the corner of the living room. He rubbed his face, looked at the clock, came over to my chair and put his arms around me from behind. "You're pitiful, you know that?" he said. I nodded. He yawned, rubbed my shoulders. "People like you just fine, as far as I can see. Look, I thought you liked giving all these parties. I thought you were eager to make new friends. It doesn't matter to me one way or another. We'll keep it to a bare minimum, how's that? If I'd wanted a socialite, I'd have married one. I married you, remember?"

I knew I was going to steal again, long before I actually did it. The pressure had been building. Mine is a chronic condition. It

192

goes into remission for long periods, then flares up again. I began spending time at the big malls—Garden State Plaza, the Fashion Center. I'd slip Catherine twenty dollars to watch the boys. What a luxury to be free of them for a couple of hours! I didn't shop so much as I wandered around, at once soothed and excited, amidst all that stuff. I'd run my hand along a rack of soft suede jackets, smile at the sight of pretty bras and underwear, the pastel colors and lace, the baskets of wallets and change purses and cigarette cases, a hundred different shades of lipstick. I'd hate it when I ran into somebody I knew, the mother of one of my kids' friends or a wife from the dinner-party circuit, because then I'd have to snap out of it, rouse myself from my private reverie, and have an ordinary conversation.

Before long I was taking note when saleswomen turned their backs on me . . . consciously playing the suburban matron . . . measuring distances between displays and exits. One day in Bamberger's I saw a silk blouse—the palest pink, with short sleeves and pearl buttons. I slipped it into my bag and walked out of the store. It was a beautiful autumn day, clear and chilly. I walked fast all the way to the other end of the mall, as far from Bamberger's as I could get. In the courtyard there was a stand that sold the most delicious hot pretzels in the world. Once I'd calmed down, I bought one, slathered it with yellow mustard, sat on a bench and devoured it.

What happens is I steal once and that starts a spree. I steal and steal and steal until I get caught. It was B. Altman's this time. I was arrested, photographed, and fingerprinted. The detective said I stole like a professional thief. John convinced the store to drop the charges by telling them I had a history of emotional instability and promising I'd get treatment.

After he'd placated the the store manager, John tried to talk to me about why I'd done it. We went for a long drive, I remember, and John asked me what was missing for me, what was he *not* doing. I was humiliated, I was contrite, I promised John I'd never do it again. I agreed to go see somebody, my first psychiatrist. Dr. Sanderson recommended hospitalization for intensive treatment.

I went to a private psychiatric hospital in Connecticut. Up there, I loved my leisure. I'd have an hour of individual therapy, another of group, and the rest of the day to myself. It was the perfect mix of company and solitude. I walked the grounds, read, worried about John and the boys far less than I thought I would. I was too busy worrying about how hot my tea was, how clean my robe, whether the other ladies would let me watch Mike Douglas or make me sit through the game shows they liked so much. John came to see me on Sundays, bringing cards from the kids and their school papers. I loved my little bed with its thick cotton sheets, one button to raise or lower my head, another to summon a nurse.

I got pregnant again in 1973 and prayed to God for a girl. There's a particular loneliness that comes from being the only female in a family. I love my husband and sons, but I'm not one of them. Americans who've lived abroad talk about pining for home, craving the sound of English, pouncing on anybody from the States. A New Yorker runs into somebody from Dallas, and they carry on like long-lost neighbors. I missed the girls from my old neighborhood in Ventnor, especially Judy. I wondered how she was, thought about calling her but didn't. I missed my mother and sister. Some days I'd be so glad to see my housekeeper come through the door—a girl! Catherine is a wonderful woman, but she's all business. She comes to my house to work, not to make friends. A few times, early on, I ate lunch with her at the kitchen table, but I could tell she was wondering if eating lunch with me would be part of her job, an additional duty. She prefers to sit and read her newspaper in peace.

A daughter, I wanted a daughter so badly. I was afraid my disappointment would be more than I could bear if the new baby was a boy. During the last couple of months of my pregnancy I stole wildly, recklessly—my promise to John fell by the wayside. It's a miracle I wasn't arrested. But, then again, who would suspect a pregnant lady wearing expensive maternity clothes and flat shoes?

When Susan was born I was ecstatic. "You have a beautiful baby daughter," the doctor said. Right there in the delivery room I swore I'd never steal another thing as long as I lived. That would be my gift to my little girl. I cupped her head in my hand and believed God and I had made a deal.

About a year later John broke the news to me that we were in serious financial trouble. Lorraine had gotten involved with a group of speculators who promised a lot more than they could deliver. When all the smoke cleared, we were nearly bankrupt. John had to sell what he could and mortgage the rest, and even then it was all he could do to keep the creditors at bay. He'd come home in the evening pale and bleary and go right for the scotch. I'd wake up in the middle of the night alone in our bed, then go from room to room until I found him, hunched over a yellow pad or arguing with his mother on the telephone.

Money trouble. All the anxiety I'd felt as a kid . . . never enough. There had never been enough money, enough food, enough beds in the house, enough jobs in the world. I felt betrayed: The Tylers were supposed to be immune from this sort of thing. How much money does a person need to be safe?

Agnes Rossi

I had to go to Newark one day, the mortgage on our house was held by a bank there and I had to give the loan officer some document or other. I got lost, drove around dilapidated streets for over an hour looking for the bank. Discount stores with their merchandise piled high in bins on the sidewalks, check-cashing places, abandoned buildings—it was just like the poorest sections of Atlantic City but on a bigger scale.

The man in the bank was terse with me, his tone clipped, his expression accusatory.

In the Bamberger's in Newark I really stood out; not many rich white ladies shopped there. The atmosphere was livelier than in the suburban store, the floor a little dirtier, the merchandise not so well tended. Many of the saleswomen were old-timers; they remembered Newark in its prime. I was just the sort of person they used to get in there back when, and they doted on me. It was the perfect setup, really. I stole a small bottle of very expensive perfume, was more daring than I'd ever been before. I had the cosmetics saleswoman show me half a dozen different items. The poor old dear was so convinced that she and I were in league against the other customers, against the general disintegration all around us, that it never occurred to her to watch my hands.

Stealing in Newark was a special pleasure. The drive down from Saddle River, the rough-and-tumble of the streets, the deference of the old Jewish salesladies, the expressions of the girls sitting on stoops, waiting at bus stops, standing in doorways with little brothers or sisters on their hips. They'd never believe I know what's inside them, but I do. I do. Never enough.

. . .

SPLIT SKIRT

Of course I felt guilty for breaking the promise I'd made in the delivery room. I'd tiptoe into the nursery at night and watch Susan sleep. Listening to her breathe, I'd quake at my own duplicity. But eventually, over time, I convinced myself that my vowing to stop for the good of my daughter had been wrong in the first place. Susan hadn't come into the world to fix me. I've always managed to find some way or other to let myself off the hook.

I'm the wife of a prominent businessman, the mother of three sons and a daughter. I'm a thief—sneaky, daring, reckless. Selfish. Don't forget selfish. You know what it feels like to me? It feels like somewhere along the way parts of my self split off from the whole. They took up in a place cut off from my circulatory system, starved for oxygen. They turned, I guess, like wine turns. They soured like milk.

It was a hard year, the worst. A few days before Christmas Lorraine discovered she had cancer in her left breast. When John came home in the middle of the day, I couldn't imagine what had happened, thought he'd suffered some crushing business failure. "My mother," he said, and his throat closed. He never called her that, always just Lorraine. He got on the phone then, talked to our doctor friends and had Lorraine moved from Atlantic City to Sloan Kettering. She had a mastectomy and radiation, but too late. A month after her surgery a tumor was discovered at the base of her skull.

The devil himself must have designed Lorraine's death. It could not have been crueler. Mutilated, just lucid enough to know she'd been duped out of the fortune she'd worked her whole life building, she was sure she could repair the damage if

197

she lived. But she knew she wasn't going to live. John sat with her as much as she'd let him. She talked about business deals that had taken place twenty years earlier, mistook him for his father, swore like a sailor. John had to have the telephone taken out of her room.

Holy God, what the loss of a charismatic mother does to a man. John's grief ran roughshod over him. The ordeal of Lorraine's illness had been too much; John couldn't get out from under the memory of those last months.

One evening I found him down in the basement going through the brown bags of Lorraine's clothes I'd packed up to be sold at a flea market to benefit Valley Hospital. Lorraine had some gorgeous things—she never scrimped on herself—and I knew the ladies at the hospital would be glad to get them. John was concentrating fiercely, had the granite focus of a crazy person. "John?" I said, and he flinched, looked disoriented for a moment, then started to yell. "These are perfectly good. You were going to give them away? What's the matter with you?" He carried every stitch of his mother's clothes up three flights to the cedar closet. He must have made a dozen trips.

Lorraine's clothes are still in my cedar closet, most of them, anyway; I've never had the heart to throw any of them out. A few years ago Susan was rummaging through the hall closets and discovered them. She was delighted—Grandma Tyler's clothes! She doesn't remember Lorraine like the boys do, but she's heard so many stories about her. Susan would come downstairs in the morning wearing one of Lorraine's Chanel skirts with a big sloppy sweater and high-top sneakers. John would tease her, but he got a kick out of it. He'd look at me smugly as if to say, See? Perfectly good.

SPLIT SKIRT

John missed his mother every single day. She'd been his business partner, his mentor, his confidante. A psychologist would have a field day with John, I know, but the fact is, outside of me and the children, he didn't have anybody. With us he was husband, father, provider. He had business associates, men he ate lunch with and played golf with, but he didn't have a single friend. John should have been able to confide in me, but he was afraid to, afraid he'd upset me, afraid I'd start up again.

I was thrown by Lorraine's death too. In a sense, I'd married John and Lorraine. I'd resented that plenty of times, but there it was. Without Lorraine, our family seemed vulnerable.

After the first period of wild grief, John got depressed. He put what energy he had into his work. Our money troubles didn't let up; I honestly don't know how John managed to hold on. He must have felt so alone while he tried to repair the damage Lorraine's final investment had caused. How many times during his workday did he want to ask his mother's advice? At home he'd sit in his study and brood, then slip into bed at two or three in the morning smelling of whiskey.

We were all afraid of him. Susan was just a toddler, and I lavished attention on her to make up for John's gruffness. We were a pair, Susan and I, but still, I worried about her. The boys I was forever shushing. David was twelve and a hotshot even then. He was starting to mouth off to me, wouldn't tell me where he was going or where he'd been. I needed John's help with him but didn't dare ask for it. John junior was fourteen and too serious, I thought. He knew there were money problems, and they frightened him. He tried to talk to John about what was happening, but John told him to mind his business, worry about algebra and chemistry. Andrew was an angel; that kid was born with the disposition of a saint. That's why I'm so willing to put up with his lack of ambition now, why I never really mind sending him money.

Agnes Rossi

Andrew should have been a girl. He'd have been pretty and pliant, and some man would have come along to take care of him. The women Andrew's been involved with all go through the same thing. They fall in love with his good looks and his gentleness, and then they swing into action, try to inspire him to do something with his life. They convince him to enroll in college, or they get him a job where they work. Six months later, Andrew has dropped out of school, been fired or quit, and the women are at their wit's end; they put him out bag and baggage.

John's grief and depression dragged on and on. I was ready to tell him he had to do something, go for help or consider moving out. I like to think that if I'd been alone, I would have been willing to hang in with John no matter what, but I couldn't stand by and let him become the sort of shadow presence my own father had been. Then, over the course of a couple of weeks, he snapped out of it. He was buoyant all of a sudden, lighthearted. He'd sneak up and put his arms around me from behind like when we were first married; he'd ask me to wait dinner for him so we could all eat together; he'd make a point of asking Susan if she wanted to go with him when he went out to run errands on Saturdays.

Then he started buying clothes for himself. John had never cared about that sort of thing before; he wore whatever his mother or I bought for him. Now salesmen from Wallachs and Brooks Brothers were calling the house to say that this or that had just come in. I was relieved and grateful; his despair had run its course. I thought too he was beginning to see daylight financially.

You know where this is going. A letter without a stamp in the mailbox, just my name on the envelope, no address. It was from a young woman who worked in John's office. She told me John had been chasing her for months. Had put his hands on her.

200

SPLIT SKIRT

She'd tried to discourage him, made it clear she wasn't interested, but he wouldn't leave her alone, claimed to be in love with her. He bought her gifts, a necklace, perfume, all of which she refused to accept. Lately he'd been calling her house at all hours, asking questions about intimate matters, using foul language. She was quitting, but she wanted me to know what my husband was up to because she was about to get married and if her husband ever did what John had done, she'd want to know. It was a tidy letter, neat secretarial script, indented paragraphs. It was signed "Very truly yours, Carol Eliason."

John didn't come in until after midnight. I handed him the letter. He glanced at it, took off his tie, and sat down on the edge of our bed. Carol was a good girl, he said; she'd come to work for him about a year ago. That afternoon she'd quit, had told him she'd written to me, said she'd go to the police if he ever bothered her again. "If you want me to leave this house tonight," he said, "I will."

I cried for three days. The thought of John trying to seduce another woman made me feel like there was blood in my stomach. I drove myself crazy imagining those late-night phone calls; he had to have made them while the kids and I were asleep. I got furious at this Carol. Was she as innocent as she claimed to be? She must have led him on, come to work in short skirts and low-cut sweaters, leaned over his desk so he could get a good look. When he'd done what any man would do, she turned on him. I'd take out the letter, read it again, and know Carol Eliason was just a girl with a lousy secretarial job and a creepy boss.

A serious negotiation started up deep inside me. It might have been different, I suppose, if he'd had an affair, slept with her. What he'd done was make a fool out of himself. He was a paunchy middle-aged man, crazy with grief for his mother, making a play for a much younger girl, strutting around in new clothes, talking dirty over the telephone to punish her for rejecting him.

I tallied up the crimes each of us had committed over the years. I had to admit I'd put John through a lot. He hadn't always been heroic, maybe, but he had stuck around. I remembered the day we brought John junior home from the hospital, remembered standing by the bassinet with John's arms around our first baby and me. I asked myself if I'd ever desert one of my kids. Could any of them do something so despicable that I'd turn away? No, of course not. I'll go on being their mother no matter what. I thought of Lorraine and her willingness to put our battles behind her for John's sake, for the sake of our family. Our lives would have been so much harder if she'd decided to make me her enemy.

· To you this may sound cold, calculated—weighing one offense against another, comparing columns on an emotional balance sheet. Maybe you think all of this is an elaborate rationalization. You think I settled. I used to wonder about that myself. But now I know I didn't. I'm telling you, I didn't settle. John deserved to be forgiven. What I have to do now, when I get home, is give him the opportunity to forgive me.

TWENTY-TWO

*T*hunder crashes overhead, the loudest I've ever heard. Mrs. Tyler puts her hands over her ears. Something must have been hit—a roof, a brick chimney, a fat oak tree. All over Bergen County dogs just dove under beds and little kids are headed down hallways.

"Dios mio," Luz whispers, and the rain pours down.

The sound is comforting here like it is everywhere; it makes you grateful for shelter. Whatever else you are, you are not out in it. Up and down the cellblock, women say yes and thank Jesus for the rain that might cool us down.

I keep thinking I'm at the beginning of my story, think I've found the place where things started to warp. Then, just as I'm congratulating myself—ah, yes, my troubles all started right here—I remember something else, something that happened much earlier, and I realize I'm not where I thought I was—not yet, anyway.

My earliest memory then, to be safe, there is nothing before it: a dream. My sisters and I making our way through the jungle, having ourselves an adventure; our voices clear when we call out, our bodies nimble as we scramble over rough terrain. We're outward bound. My dreaming a safari is not as unlikely as it sounds. Our favorite cartoon was *Jungle Boy*. He could have been one of us. Impish, tan, he had dark hair too long for a boy back then; he even had bangs like we did. When he did his herky-jerky dance with the elephants, we danced too, all around the den.

My mother didn't believe little girls needed shirts in the summertime, so we ran around bare-chested. There were eight of us, remember—eight half-naked girls. Some neighborhood brothers—called us natives when we fought them for time on the rope swing that hung in the woods between our backyard and theirs.

A rope swing? Phallic, right? That rope swing was a great penis we wanted so desperately we were willing to fight older boys for it. Wrong. I was there, and I know. We swung on that rope because it was scary and fun. Grab it, pull it all the way up the incline, position the knot between your legs, and push off. The rope felt good so close to my box because it rubbed a spot there to be rubbed, not because it was the penis I'd been born without.

Having only sisters and a father who was the soul of modesty, I was older than most girls when I saw my first penis. At a family gathering a younger cousin came out of the bathroom asking to have his pants pulled up please. What *is* that? I was curious, to be sure, but not envious. My cousin's penis looked soft and vulnerable. I was embarrassed for it and for him. Maybe if I'd seen one under more flattering circumstances, I'd have been impressed. But nobody looks enviable walking with his pants down around his ankles.

The next penises I saw were in a book on a bottom shelf at home, called *Vietnam Doctor*. Whenever I was in a certain mood and nobody else was around, I'd flip to the photographs of naked little Vietnamese boys. Their penises between their legs made me think of webbed fingers, the wing skin of bats or flying squirrels. I thought it must be frustrating for them never to be able to spread their legs fully, to have all that hanging matter in the way. Interest, warm interest, sent me back to that book again and again. Titillation but not a desire to sprout a penis of my own. A few years later in gym class I learned to do a split and was grateful for the clean spread, the V. Even now, I swear, when Alex lolls around our bedroom naked, his penis slack against his thigh, I think it must be a bother to have to arrange himself so carefully. What a pain it would be if I had to move my liver over just a smidge closer to my small intestine before I rolled onto my side.

Whenever we spot a difference, don't we naturally assume we're the standard and the other the deviation? Occidental/Oriental eyes. Negro/Caucasian hair. If martians landed in Times Square tomorrow and they had goldfish protruding from their foreheads, would we all develop goldfish envy?

"What were you like as a kid, Rita? You were a tomboy, I'll bet."

"You'd lose. I was the girliest girl going, Mrs. Tyler. I was your sister Margie all over again."

This is going to sound strange, but bear with me. I was a very pretty little girl. You know how models and movie stars always say they were not beautiful children? They were gawky and gangly and nobody gave them a second look. The old ugly-duckling, graceful-swan business. Reverse the order, and you've got my story. I was a doll. Friends of my parents would single me out and pull me onto their laps. An old neighbor man told me I looked like Theresa Brewer, told me and told me and told me the way old men will. I didn't know who Theresa Brewer was—I still don't—but my mother seemed pleased. He'd pinch my cheek with fingers that smelled of the bug spray he put on his roses.

When I was eight years old I was riding on an escalator in a department store listening to a man lecture a woman about using too much makeup. He pointed to me as an example of natural beauty. "Look at that," he said. "Gorgeous and perfectly clean." The woman was a willing student. She stared; I opened my eyes wide, shook my head so my hair fell back from my face, sucked in my cheeks. I was so thoroughly caught up in being pretty, I didn't notice the step I was standing on flattening. I lost my footing, fell, cut my lip on corrugated metal.

A few years ago I was in an airport carrying one big suitcase in each hand. I tried to step onto the escalator without letting go of either bag, but I could not do it. My heart raced and I felt dizzy, as if I were looking down from a great height. The people behind me got huffy, so I sent one suitcase on ahead.

Because of the attention I got, I tapped into the whole male/female dynamic way early. Starting in first grade, I had fervent boyfriends. They wrote me notes, gave me quarters. One boy threw rocks at our house because I wouldn't go steady with him. Another boy's mother called mine to say that at first she thought her son's crush on me was cute but the whole thing had gone too far; her boy wasn't himself anymore. He made me an elaborate Valentine's Day card full of heat and yearning. I walked around for days with that card in the waistband of my underwear.

A teenaged cousin had a friend who invited me to sit between them in the front seat of the car, called me his baby, leered at me while I ran around with the other kids at a barbecue pretending to play tag. Yeah, right. I couldn't have cared less who was it. My attention was at the table with Freddy.

After our bath one night, Eva and I slipped out the back door and sat down on the cement steps naked. We squirmed, giggled, leaned into each other, bumped heads. Then being outside nude wasn't enough. We started yelling to the older boy who lived behind us. Eva would shout his name, and I'd clap my hand over her mouth for as long as I could stand her tongue on my palm, and then we'd switch. I'd shout and she'd silence me. Our neighbor didn't hear us, but my older sister did. She ran and told my mother. Eva and I were smacked on our way in and sent to bed sniffling and accusing each other. We lay still and listened while my mother headed upstairs to tell Dad. "We're dead, dead, dead," Eva whispered. Our room was right below our parents'. We heard our names in a sputtering story, waited to hear footsteps. My mother's voice trailed off, then my father started to laugh. "Jesus Christ," he said. "It's forty-five degrees out there."

I used to listen to pop music on AM radio and get all worked up. What's your name, who's your daddy—a man asking a girl what she knows about sex. A sound like cymbals crashing but muffled. I couldn't wait to turn sixteen; I thought that was the magic number. When I turned sixteen, boys in sport jackets would be coming for me in their convertibles.

The first indication that I wasn't going to continue being belle of the ball: other girls started developing breasts. I saw swells under their shirts and sore-looking nipples at slumber parties, and knew I was in for a bad time. My own nipples were inert, still and sterile as dimes.

Agnes Rossi

Certain boys had it in for me. During my years as a popular and sought-after girl, I'd been conceited and rude. "Carpenter's dream," they said now that breasts were part of the equation, "flat as a board." "Pirate's dream, a sunken chest." There was a kid I'd dubbed Fatboy; I'd called him that once at the bus stop in fifth grade, and it stuck. He came back at me now with the more original if not very graceful "two raisins on an ironing board." In eighth grade our teacher played a dictionary game with us in which she'd read a definition, and we'd have to guess the word. In a championship bout, one whole class against another, she said, "A flat, three-sided—" and a boy jumped up and said, "Rita."

Imagine if the size of a boy's developing penis were immediately apparent to everybody. They wag them at one another in locker rooms and sneak peeks at urinals, I know, but suppose every girl in school knew so-and-so had a little one; suppose there were antic nicknames and amusing puns—dimple dick, a monkey's dream, a small organ. We'd have many more mass murderers on our hands.

Eyyyy, adolescence. My skin broke out, my features changed. It turned out I had my father's nose and deep-set eyes and a weak chin. I wasn't pretty anymore. I know, I know, I'm not exactly Quasimodo, but don't miss the point. The world didn't welcome me the way it once had. I'd lost my authority, my source of power. Boys could take me or leave me. One well-meaning if ambivalent high school boyfriend told me he'd had enough of bitchy beauty queens and was glad to be with a girl like me. One night we were watching a rerun of *The Ed Sullivan Show*. The Beatles were on. My boyfriend looked at Ringo Starr drumming

SPLIT SKIRT

away all big-nosed and goofy and said, "Hey, Rita. He looks like you!"

It wasn't just boys. Girls treated me differently too. They didn't dote on me the way they once had, didn't vie for my attention. My insolence wasn't charming anymore. Pretty is as pretty does, my ass. Pretty girls are tyrants. They can behave any old way they choose, and people still want to be friends with them. But a haughty demeanor and a plain face make a girl very unpopular.

So what's the moral of the story? Stay pretty, and you'll be safe in this world? No, no, no. Go back to the dream of girls fending for themselves in the jungle. Back to the little Chinese girl who's not available to be made crazy by her crazy father, to Marisol saying you're teaching me to swim, Rita, I'm learning how to swim. The trouble starts with pretty.

TWENTY-THREE

I never tell a john my real name. It's bad luck to. I say Darlene, the name I use when I dance. White boys never heard of Luz anyway. When I used to tell, they always thought I said L, O, S, E or *loose,* ha ha, very funny.

Sometimes I like to be locked up. I get upset, so I like to be locked up to think things over. It's not bad here, believe me. Passaic County, now that's a different story. But here it's not so bad.

My grandmother raised me. I lived with her from the time I was born, just about. I love her dearly to this day, I don't hold no grudges, but I had to get out. That's all, wasn't her fault, wasn't my fault. She was too strict, didn't let me do nothing I wanted to do. I have a sister three years older. Idalia is nice and quiet and does good in school. Me, I was bad from the jump. If you ask my grandmother, I mean.

Idalia and me have different fathers. My mother was married to Idalia's. He was a bus driver, straight, but my mother run off with my father the junkie, Mr. Slick. Last I heard he was sick and some lady was taking care of him in New York. My father's small and skinny. My grandmother looked at me, saw him.

My mother, now she was a little wild herself. She hurt my grandmother bad. Nana was determined that me and Idalia wasn't going to go like my mother. From the time I was small, Nana wouldn't speak my mother's name, say she don't have no daughter, only granddaughters. I wanted to do my eyes up, wear high heels, but Nana wouldn't let me. And our house was so quiet, bor-ring. My grandmother kept pictures of Jesus and Mary all over the place. She love Mary, that's her girl. Those pictures look sad in the daytime, but they start looking scary at night. My grandmother, she drag me to church, squeeze my hand hard till I pull it away, shake it.

Seem like I was always in trouble. I had a bad attitude, I admit, couldn't stand nobody telling me what to do. I would do the opposite for spite.

I was twelve years old when I first had sex. This boy named Wilfredo lived downstairs. He look good. Real good. Seventeen years old, black hair, built, one hoop in his ear, white white teeth. He didn't want no part of me at first for the fact I was so young. He told me to get lost, treated me like a kid. But I just kept hanging around, and pretty soon he start messing with me. Nana caught us up on the roof and gave me a beating, told Wilfredo's mother she would call the cops if he ever come near me again. Right away Will went in the army. When he come home for a visit he talk to me like a damn gym teacher.

SPLIT SKIRT

Going with boys was something to do. I liked it. In their cars. In their beds when their mothers wasn't around. Back then it was exciting to me, better than the stuff Idalia was always doing, talking on the phone to her friends, going downtown and looking at clothes, dancing in our room with the door closed. I could not be bothered with none of that.

Some of the boys I went with badmouthed me behind my back. The same motherfuckers calling me up talking about please, please, please. Girls fucking their boyfriend and his brother every night of the week talking shit about me. Idalia come home and called me a slut, said was I happy now I had a reputation. Why you got to be so dirty, Luz? What's wrong with you?

Idalia's all right though. I hated her back then for being so good. But now I'm proud of my sister. She's going to college, taking up business administration. Idalia's going to marry some nice straight man, have a hundred and fifty kids. Nana deserve Idalia after what she went through with my mother and me. Idalia couldn't make it out here anyway. She soft, don't know the first thing about taking care of herself outside. I'm three years younger but yet and still when Idalia had trouble with somebody, she'd come and tell me, and I'd fight them. Small as I am, girls was scared of me back then. I'd fight anybody mess with my sister.

I used to say could I just do what I want to do and everybody leave me alone. Every day I was in trouble somewhere, at home or at school. I was going with boys, getting high, staying out nights, all that. I skipped school one day, come home to find a white lady sitting on the couch. She look like you, Rita, she look better than you. The judge in juvenile court said I was incorrigible, sentenced me to six weeks in Conklin. I begged my grand-

213

mother to keep me home, give me one more chance. But she had enough of my bullshit. Better you cry now than I cry later, she said.

Conklin was a trip. Crack patients, drunks, girls cut themselves with razor blades for nothing. One mess took a hammer and broke every window in her house, then smash her own hand. I was keeping to myself, counting my days, when this older girl named Beth start talking to me. She called me chippie for giving it away on the outside. You might as well get paid, she said.

Tricks like young girls because we're tight. If a man's worried about having a little one, he thinks it'll be big inside a baby. And pay for it too. I get twice what Madeline gets, easy. I'm smaller and prettier too. Pretty gets you paid.

Beth told me about a bar in Teterboro where I could make one hundred dollars a night dancing. GIRLS, GIRLS, GIRLS, the sign over the door said. Inside it was dark, and a couple of girls was dancing to loud club music. The bartender looked at me and jerked his head, meaning what do you want, you know. He was tall, asshole Eddie with a beard, think he's hot shit because he's behind the bar. I said I was a dancer. He look me up and down, say you ever dance before. In Florida, I told him, which is what Beth told me to say.

The back room was filthy dirty. I'll never forget. A metal desk covered with papers and ashtrays and glasses, two chairs with seats look like they been slashed with a knife. A white guy behind the desk, with red hair, metal glasses, his shirt stretched over his fat gut. He told me to turn around, ask how old I was. Eighteen. You got I.D.? Not on me. He didn't say nothing, pulled up my shirt, pinched my tit. He said give a blow job and I could dance.

I made forty-seven dollars in tips that night, just dancing. Fifteen minutes on, fifteen minutes off, and bouncers make sure nobody touches you. I didn't have no place to go when the bar closed, so one of the girls said I could stay with her. She had a big old apartment over a florist. She put me in a room that was full of junk, boxes, and piles of old clothes. Wasn't no heat in there, it was freezing cold, and I couldn't sleep thinking how I was all on my own now, no Nana, no Idalia, no even Conklin. My legs was twitching from the cold and from so much dancing, and I was scared, but I knew if I was to go back home, I wouldn't last a month before I would get in trouble and Nana would put me out again. I rather be on my own than back in Conklin or in some damn group home. I think of it like this: Being how I am, I'm better off on the street.

It was pitch black in that room, so dark it didn't make not one bit of difference if my eyes was open or shut. Freezing cold too. I curled myself up so I was small as I could be, pulled the blanket over my head. You ever start to fall asleep but don't know it till you hear a snore and you think what the fuck is that, but it's you? The sound you're hearing is you.

TWENTY-FOUR

*I*n the morning Rita and Mrs. Tyler open their eyes a split second before one kitchen worker calls out to another. Somehow, in their sleep, they heard him take a deep breath, open his mouth. "Salt," he bellows. "Now stirrrrrrr."

They're getting out today. Out. Soon.

Like long-married people who've booked a bargain flight and must leave for the airport before dawn, Rita and Mrs. Tyler wash and dress without a word. Throat-clearing, tooth-brushing, tamping down clothes in bags; noises stand in for speech this morning.

It was nearly three o'clock when Rita and Mrs. Tyler and Luz said good night. Rita's fingers tremble tying the laces of her sneakers. Short sleep, big day. In the brew of exhilaration, anxiety, dread, a question swims back and forth, methodically, like a businessman doing his laps in the pool at the Y. Will Alex be waiting for me when I step outside?

Mrs. Tyler slept soundly. Her head is clear, her hands are steady. She combs her hair straight back—no teasing, no hair spray. She's thinking about standing under the shower in her own bathroom, washing her hair twice, scrubbing her skin with a washcloth, shaving her legs, rubbing her best lotion all over; about the private pleasure of dressing slowly, carefully, to spend the evening alone with John. Maybe we'll get in the car, she thinks, and drive out to the country in Pennsylvania. We could take a ride down to the Jersey shore. Maybe it would be better if we just spend the time at home. Yes, that's what we'll do. She cannot wait to cook dinner in her own kitchen, to sit outside with John as the daylight softens, then fades, to lie down on clean cotton sheets.

Dressed, packed, ready to go, Rita and Mrs. Tyler sit on their cots, bags on their laps, and wait.

Finally a guard comes, puts her key in the lock, says, "Shall we?"

Out they go, Rita first.

Madeline stands near the bars of her cell, her face bloated from sleep, bedhead. Rita and Mrs. Tyler stop. The guard, who's in no hurry to complete this task and get on to the next, indulges them. Madeline clears her throat, runs her hands through her hair. Mrs. Tyler says goodbye, you . . . you be careful. Madeline smiles drowsily and says be good.

Luz, meanwhile, is sound asleep, curled on her side, head on the crook of her elbow, hand between her knees. Rita stands right up against the bars and takes a last look at Luz. Small feet, the grime that comes from wearing shoes without socks or stockings, a string of purple beads around one ankle, black hair on skinny legs, short skirt. Luz's chest rises and falls steadily, easily, like any girl asleep, Rita thinks, like any kid. She stares at the bow of Luz's upper lip, at her long, dark eyelashes. Little sister, Rita thinks. "Will you tell her I said goodbye?"

There are official release procedures, the return of their watches and wallets and wedding rings. The bathos of the last— it slides out of the manila envelope, clatters on the counter— makes Rita frown. The trouble with symbols, she thinks. She's about to put the ring in her pocket, but slips it on her finger instead. She knows she may end up throwing it off a bridge but would hate to plain lose it, to tap her pocket and discover it gone. They sign three papers apiece, then walk out a side door and are free.

Just like that.

The moment is murky and ordinary. They'd waited for this, here it comes, where the hell did it go? The ground is spongy, the air smells of wet grass, dirt, and pavement. Squinting in the sun, they walk around to the front of the jail.

No Alex.

A couple of police cars, yes, a station wagon with New York plates, the arc of the circular drive, and insipid flowers, pink, yellow, and white.

But no Alex.

Rita bites her bottom lip. Wait and see, she thinks.

At the curb they're suddenly shy. Rita puts her hands in her pockets. Mrs. Tyler tugs at the ends of her sleeves.

"I don't want to leave you alone here, Rita. My car's in a garage just down the street. I'll take you wherever you want to go. Come with me, please."

"No. I'm going to wait here a few minutes. If Alex doesn't come, I'll walk over to town and get a bus or a cab."

"If he were coming, sweetie, he'd be here."

"I'm not stupid," Rita says, lowering her head and crossing

her arms. "I know he probably isn't coming, but I have to be sure."

"Of course. Of course you do."

Rita puts her arms around Mrs. Tyler and remembers, instantly, tactilely, that is to say, her ribs remember, her belly and breasts do, how Mrs. Tyler had come and found her down in the dark basement. Down there. The screaming seconds when she was sure the guards had come back. Going limp with relief when she recognized the voice saying, *It's me, it's me.* Mrs. Tyler's body is soft but solid, sturdy in the daylight.

So tall, Mrs. Tyler thinks, running her hand down Rita's long spine. She hugs hard, puts her head on Rita's shoulder. In the raw physicality of the moment, body-to-body—it's been a long, hot three days without much soap and water—Mrs. Tyler understands the source of her clear head and steady hands this morning. I told Rita the truth, she thinks. I said here is what I did, here is how I felt. And I listened. She quakes at the thought of all she would have missed if she hadn't been sent to jail and feels grateful to fate, to the cosmos, to the morning sun on River Street in Hackensack, New Jersey, for providing.

"You should go now," Rita says, pulling free.

Mrs. Tyler looks into Rita's eyes, nods her head. She wants to argue, to insist that Rita leave with her, but she doesn't. Rita's instincts are good, Mrs. Tyler thinks. Maybe Rita knows it's time for them to say goodbye.

Mrs. Tyler kisses Rita, squeezes her hand, then turns resolutely and walks away, her red bag slung over her shoulder.

"Bye," Rita calls out.

Mrs. Tyler raises one arm in a wave but doesn't turn around.

. . .

220

SPLIT SKIRT

How long to wait for Alex? Fifteen minutes, Rita decides, no more. She sits down on the curb, rubs the back of her neck, checks her watch. The verdict, she knows perfectly well, is already in. The sentence she understands in a flash, as long as it takes to press the heels of her hands against her closed eyes.

There will be rage, late-night litanies absolving her of all blame, real tears and drunken jags, the merciless scrape of rejection. Lapses will suggest a breakdown is coming. She'll lose her keys several times, her wallet, will leave milk on the table when she goes to work in the morning. Her teakettle will boil dry, scorch.

Missing him will be the worst of it. Pining. There will be a couple of humiliating phone calls to his office that she'll know she shouldn't make as she pushes buttons on a pay phone. A final roll in the hay that will leave them both unspeakably sad. A battle over the house, then, to strengthen everybody's resolve.

She'll have to live every miserable second of it. But she'll get through it. In time she'll begin to feel better. She'll be older, yes, and chastened, perhaps; there will be shadows where there weren't any before, dark patches. That's how it goes, Rita thinks. Experience shouldn't just wash over us. Who can you be but who you've become?

Traffic on River Street is brisk, morning rush. Rita finds herself watching a stoplight that has outlived its usefulness. Whatever it was that once generated traffic on the cross street no longer exists. A simple stop sign would do now. When the light turns red, dozens of cars sit and wait for nothing. Some of the drivers turn and look over at Rita idly. Those close enough to see the bruises on her face stare. Under different circumstances Rita might feel self-conscious, wonder what these people on their way to work think of a woman with a fat lip and a black eye. But this morning she's just glad to be free to get up and walk when she's ready.

She'd anticipated this waiting, knew Alex wouldn't show. She'd thought she'd be anxious in the worst scalded-stomach way and had dreaded the tight throat, the shallow breaths. What she is, it turns out, is hungry. When the time's up, not much longer now, she'll buy a newspaper, eat a big breakfast—scrambled eggs, an English muffin with butter and jelly, what the hell, bacon. She'll walk over to Main Street, up to Pheiffers where the coffee is decent and she can hole up in a booth, get her bearings and decide what to do next.

She's lightheaded when she stands up. I need to walk, she thinks. Ahhhhhhhhh, the stretch of tendons between hip bones and thighs feels so good. The sidewalk is crowded, and she steps into the street. People hurry past. They smell good, Rita notices, many of them. The men's shirts are blazing white, the collars crisp; the women's lipstick is fresh, their skirts not yet wrinkled. You have to go to work and I don't, Rita thinks. If Rita's house were to catch fire, she would, after the fact, up to her ankles in sooty water, be secretly grateful for a couple of days off.

A cream-colored Cadillac passes much too close. Rita jumps onto the sidewalk, curses, glares, then recognizes the back of Mrs. Tyler's head. The blinker goes on; the Cadillac pulls into the gravel lot of a discount liquor store. The window on the passenger side glides down.

Rita walks over and leans in. "What?" she says.

Mrs. Tyler looks at Rita for a moment. "Will you stop being ridiculous?" she says finally. "Will you get in this damn car?"

The love in Mrs. Tyler's voice sounds suspiciously like pity to Rita. She bristles, her stomach tightens. "Look," she says angrily. Pausing to select a response that will send Mrs. Tyler speeding back to Saddle River, Rita stares, loses momentum, stalls. She finds herself grinning at the sight of her cellmate behind the wheel of such a fancy car.

"Are you hungry, Mrs. Tyler?" Rita says, opening the car door. "You want to get something to eat?"

ABOUT THE AUTHOR

AGNES ROSSI was born and raised in New Jersey. A graduate of Rutgers and New York University, she lives in New York City with her husband, Daniel Conaway.

ABOUT THE TYPE

This book was set in Times Roman, designed by Stanley Morison specifically for *The Times* of London. The typeface was introduced in the newspaper in 1932. Times Roman has had its greatest success in the United States as a book and commercial typeface, rather than one used in newspapers.